Prominent Afghan Women
throughout History

with

Illustrations from Ancient to Modern Times

Fawzia Abass Etemadi

i

Copyrights © 2023

In Loving Memory of My Mother,

Amena Abass

Dedicated to All the Women of Afghanistan

PREFACE

Prominent Afghan Women throughout History reflects my love for the women of Afghanistan. One of my goals in writing this book is to encourage and lift the spirits of all the women of my homeland who have suffered immeasurable mental anguish and physical brutality as a result of all the devastating wars waged during the past four decades.

Despite all odds, Afghan women's involvement and active participation in the fields of poetry, artistic creation, economic growth, politics, and struggle for independence are remarkable and noteworthy feats. The compelling force behind writing this book was to capture this rich history.

I was privileged to travel to small towns and villages in Afghanistan to gain firsthand information about Afghan women outside the metropolises. In addition to raising children, these women have always been involved in providing financial support for their families through such activities as carpet weaving, embroidering, knitting, farming, and animal husbandry.

The inspiration for writing this book was my eyewitness accounts, but most importantly the meaningful conversations I had with notable women throughout Afghanistan. Indeed, their intelligence, tolerance, bravery, resilience, perseverance and, above all, their love of country were immensely touching and left an indelible impression on me. I was most struck by the basic and fervent desire of these hardworking women to have peace and security in their homeland.

Every effort has been made to base all facts throughout this work on available, well researched, authentic historical documents. This book provides a backdrop for better understanding the social and cultural role of Afghan women in society. These women have left long-lasting impressions to this day. Their impactful roles in advancing the cause of women have won the respect and admiration of all Afghans.

It is my hope that this research will contribute to enhance understanding of these historical figures and to inspire future generations to persevere by reminding them of the glorious history and legacy of women in Afghanistan.

FawziaAbass Etemadi
Alexandria, Virginia

EDITOR'S REMARKS

Much has been written about Afghan women's activities and achievements but not in a systematic or chronological order, and on the whole, not in a way that could be considered a fair representation of them. Many writers have focused on a select group of Afghan women while leaving out others, focusing on geographic location, political orientation, linguistic or ethnic background.

Women in the "Prominent Afghan Women throughout History", is an astute and comprehensive account of the lives of outstanding Afghan women within the vast and varied regions of the country from ancient times to the present.

Meticulous and comprehensive in her research, FawziaAbass Etemadi has uncovered historical facts about Afghan women not previously known or acknowledged. Her work contributes to enhanced understanding of numerous determined, inspiring female personalities, particularly those who played key leadership roles in government and politics; patriotism and struggles for independence; and art, literature, and architecture. Afghan women also played important roles in the economic development of their regions in farming, carpet weaving, making pottery, and other handicrafts.

As she traveled through Afghanistan, Fawzia A. Etemadi drew from diverse sources, including historical Afghan national archives, discussions with historians, artists, scholars, and eminent writers. This has enabled her to paint vivid pictures of the lives, challenges and triumphs of these historical figures—pictures that enable one to appreciate the pivotal roles Afghan women have played. Good examples of these determined women are: Raihana Ghaznawid, the first Afghan woman mathematician, Al-Biruni's faithful follower: Princess Malak Mah Banu, who built the Madrassa or Grand Academy of Badghis; and other key female personalities such as Queen Halima who played varied and vital roles in building gardens, mosques, palaces and bridges.

Most importantly, Fawzia A. Etemadi covers the stories of women with no bias toward ethnic background, religious orientation, or geographic origin. The book offers a fascinating journey through centuries of Afghan women's history, their trials and tribulations, and their involvement and support for all elements of civilization. Their brave and determined efforts and contributions make them excellent role models for current and future leaders concerned about the welfare of their societies.

Ahad Shahbaz

ACKNOWLEDGEMENT

With much love to my entire family and my dear friends who have been a great support during the entire process of writing this book over the last few years.

Special thanks to Ahad Shahbaz who patiently and with a great deal of dedication and professionalism worked with me on editing the manuscript; and of course, Trina Shahbaz, his lovely wife for eloquent translation of Zarghuna Anna, and Ayesha Durrani's poems.

My deep appreciation to Malal Nezam, author of numerous articles on the vital role of women in Afghanistan, for her friendship, collegiality, and support from the very beginning of this undertaking,

Many thanks to DorkhaniZahin, the editor chief of Lemar Magazine who formatted and printed the Dari edition of this book, for her enthusiasm and remarkable professionalism,

Last but not least, I owe a great debt of gratitude to Mr. Hamid Naweed for his artistic contributions, especially designing the cover page of this book, which is based on the 15th century Kamaluddin Behzad's, painting.

ABOUT THE AUTHOR

Fawzia Etemadi received her Master's in International Relations degree from George Washington University. She studied immigration regulations at Law Enforcement Academy of Glencoe, Georgia.

 Born and raised in Afghanistan, she was forced to immigrate to the United States due to the Soviet invasion of Afghanistan in 1979. Since her arrival in the US, she has worked in different organizations, including Afghan Community in Washington DC and Afghanistan Foundation and Universal Peace Federation UPF. An advocate forpeace (Ambassador for Peace), she often speaks to large groups of women of many different cultures and nationalities.

Having been involved in cross-cultural training and discussions, she continues to be in close contact with her homeland, sharing her knowledge and expertise in various cross-cultural settings with all those concerned about the welfare of Afghans in Afghanistan and abroad.

It is her hope that this book will further contribute to increased understanding of Afghanistan, Afghan women, and their legacy.

Table of Contents

INTRODUCTION:

Looking back on the distant past in human life, from cave-dwelling to the agricultural eras, we find that women have played a valuable role in most human societies. In my research on this book, I came across "A Historical Guide to Afghanistan," by the renowned American historian and archeologist, Nancy Dupree. Her scientific discovery and recording of the existence of early humans in Afghanistan fascinated me. I learned that about one hundred thousand years ago humans lived in the plains of Dashti-Nawor near Ghazni, Afghanistan, and that women's activities, especially after the discovery of fire, had become more vital, indicating the more active roles women played in the social life of that era.

As I continued with my research on early human life, I discovered that the inhabitants of early societies were in fact very intelligent. They were able to live under the most severe conditions and environmental limitations in order to survive. In the 1960s and 1970s, however, most scientists thought that prehistoric humans were nothing more than primitive hunters and food gatherers, and that women were captives of men. The tools and other evidence of this period show that they in fact played an equal role in the development of social life.

In ancient times, men and women worked side by side in order to survive in their harsh environments. Some studies indicate that in early agrarian societies, women played even a more important role than men in their daily lives.

CHAPTER ONE

A Glance at the Social Status of Women in
Prehistoric Afghanistan& Ariana Civilizations

In the early ages, circa 10,000 BC, the situation in today's Afghanistan was similar to the rest of ancient human societies. The artifacts that have been discovered in northern and southern provinces such as Balkh, Badakhshan, Samangan, Takhar, Faryab, Laghman, Kandahar and Nuristan reveal the existence of the first human communities in this ancient land. [1]

Ancient Figurins&Potrry, Courtesy of National Museum of Afghanistan

The artifacts of this era exhibited in the National Museum of Afghanistan clearly demonstrate the way of life of these ancient people; women played a major role in agriculture dating back to eight to ten thousand years ago. A good number of these

---

[1] *Mehdizadah Kabuli, Pre Historic Afghanistan, Mashhad, first edition - 2002*

findings, including pottery and statuettes of farm animals are believed to be created by women since men were preoccupied with hunting, fighting, plowing, animal husbandry, and guarding farmlands.

By looking at the lifestyle of the Stone Age people, we find that women were very active in that period: raising children, cooking, forming, and preparing clothes from animal wool and skin. As a result, women gradually gained more social status in this era. The statues of Mother Goddess related to the Stone Age and early agrarian societies found in different parts of the country attest to this fact.

Studies by the American scholars Lewis Dupree and Alexander Marshack show that the oldest barley and wheat fields were located at the banks of Kokcha and Amu Darya rivers in northern Afghanistan. Archeological research shows that both men and women were working in these ancient farms. At the same time, a similar agricultural culture has been in an advanced stage in the southwest of Afghanistan along the Helmand and Arghandab rivers. The statues of peasant women and men from this period that were discovered from Mandigak in Kandahar prove this view.

Nancy Dupri says in this regard:

The Mother Goddess
Statue from Sothern
Afghanistan

"Early agricultural villages in Afghanistan appeared around 5000 BC, or 7000 years ago in the Kandahar region. **Deh Merasi Hill** is the first prehistoric site in Afghanistan that has been excavated so far and is located 27 kilometers southwest of Kandahar. At the same time during this period, the houses of the peasants were built with mud and mud buildings with several rooms in "Said Qala". Also, the works related to the second millennium BC, such as primitive prehistoric jewelry, clay and metal seals in the nearby place, called "**The Sword of the Cave**" were found."[2]

The statue of the mother goddess, preserved in the National Museum of Afghanistan, along with a number of very old jewelry belonging to influential

---

[2] Nancy Dupree "A Historical Guid to Afghanistan" P. 22 -24, Kabul 1977

and wealthy women of this period, tells the important role of women, from Kandahar to Zaranj. It is believed that in this period, the idea of women and land as sources of production was the general belief. Thus, women became the personification of prosperity and comfort in this era. Because of the belief in earth and mother as two holy elements, it established the foundation of ancient religions. According to the scientific findings, most scientists are of the opinion that this era can be called the era of Matriarchy.[3]

The Roleof Women in the Era of Vedic and Avestan Civilizations:

Based on historical studies, the land ancient Ariana was the cradle of early civilization; the delicate statuests of women, which are discovered from the cultural Basin of Amo- Darya (the Oxus River), Margab in northern Afghanistan and Merv in the southern parts of Turkmenistan, are ample examples that prove this observation. These ancient artifacts show the civilized and cultured way of life of early urban societies, which flourished during the Bronze Age in this area. Although we don't know if these artifacts were made by women or men, these historical figurines express the fact that around 2,500 to 3,000 years before the birth of Christ, women had great influence and importance in the ancient Bactrian culture. Their fine, delicate costumes, hairstyle and neatness of their general appearance show that

people of Balkh, Marghab and Marv lived a prosperous and civilized way of life; and women had a considerable social status at that time. Also, the statues of the Mother Goddesses from the south of Kandahar indicate the same importance of women in the ancient times.

SstoneStatuets of "Bactrian Women" Louvre Museum, Paris

According to the research of

[3]Neumann, Erich (1991). The Great Mother, Bollingen; Repr/7th edition. Princeton University Press, Princeton, NJ

5

the famous German historian and linguist Michael Witzel, most of the Rigvida prayers were told by women. Here are some examples of the short poems of these female poets:

Poems from Rigvida told by Women

From the slopes of gentle and snowy mountains
Two galloping mares
The crystal bases are sharp
And two bright mother cows
Who follow their calves,
They bring the waters down rapidly.
****

Gods, we fail at nothing,
And we don't want to hide anything.
While we want to follow your advice,
We stand together with the strength of our capable shoulders.

Perhaps for this reason, the role of women is strongly evident in the Vedic hymns, especially in the Rigveda, and also in the Gathas hymns in the book of Avesta. As previously mentioned, the statues of the mother goddess from the south of Kandahar express the same notion. Perhaps for this reason, the role of women can be seen in the Vedic hymns, especially in the Rigveda, and in the Gathas in the Avesta.

During the migration of the Aryan tribes from Balkh towards the Indian subcontinent circa 1800 BC, the Vedic hymns told the oral history of the Aryan people. Later these ancient hymns were written in Sanskrit language. According to Michael Witzil, women in this period chose to consider family life important. These women were called "Sadivados" and were always active in the service of the community.

Regarding the social activities of ancient Aryans and the role of women in society, Professor Ahmad Ali Khan Kohzad, prominent Afghan historian, mentions that in the ancient Aryan civilization, women played an active role. Wedding ceremonies were held in a special glorious manner with instruments and Attan (special Afghan dance) and, of course, horse racing competitions. These ceremonies are still common

in almost all villages of Afghanistan today. Below is a couplet from the Ancient Aryans wedding song, sung by a bride to her groom during their wedding ceremony?
Is it possible that the gods of the waters join our hearts?
Could the winds of the mountains bring us closer?

It can, therefore, safely be said that the active role of women in the Ariana civilization had an amazing importance in both Vedic and Avestan epochs.

During the reign of the (Apa-gan) the Aspa Dynasty of Balkh, names of many important ladies have been mentioned in Avestan texts, including Doghda, Zoroaster's mother, Hui, his wife, and Pourjaspa, his daughter. They were real personalities to be remembered. However, Anahita, the guardian of the flowing waters, Shabana, the first woman in the world, and Jahika, the daughter of the devil, were all mythical figures. In any case, all these names reflect the importance, presence, and roles of women in Avestan culture.

In contrast, in the Mesopotamian civilization and Achaemenids culture, men had more power. In the cultures of this area, most of the sculptures show influential figures of powerful men. The large statues of men's bodies and men's heads and long-bearded faces with winged bulls and lions symbolize men's power and dominance. This imposing artwork reflects the culture of patriarchy, pointing out the start of the culture of patriarchy in this region.

Fables of Legendary Women in Ancient Ariana

In the Avestan culture, most myths tell the stories of women. For example, "Varizkna," as mentioned in Avesta or "Behafrid" as described in the verses of Firdausi, was the daughter of King Visht-Aspt also known as Gesht-Asp, the ruler of Balkh. She was an influential and faithful princess who made great efforts in spreading the Avestan religion and spreading the culture of good deeds. It is said that the Roshan Fire Temple in Kabul was built by her.

The stories of Shahnamah(The Epics of Kings) by Firdausi, the 11th century poet in the court of Sultan Mahmud of Ghazni, describes Sindukht as another famous woman who saved the city of Kabul from destruction during the battle between Sam, the great warrior of all times, and Mehrab, the ruler of Kabul.

The Shahnamah describes Sam as the great warrior of all times who was about to attack Kabul with his mighty army from Zabulistan, (the province between today's Kabul and Ghazni). Sindukht tried to find a solution to stop the war and save Kabul from destruction. In Shahnama, Firdausi reveals the impact of Sindukht on the impending war and her strategy for achieving peace. The great hero, Sam, was extremely upset with Mehrab, the ruler of Kabul and wanted to punish Merab with his large army, preparing for the attack from Zabul. Sindukht, Mehrab's wife, was the queen of Kabul. She had a kind personality and loved her people. In order to save the city of Kabul from war and destruction, she proposed to Mehrab that she would see Sam in person for peace and reconciliation before any war breaks out. Mehrab confidently accepted his wife's advice. Sindukht prepared the most valuable gifts such as precious jewels, excellent breeds of horses, the highest quality swords, and elephants.

After careful preparations, Sindukht rode on her galloping horse and rushed to Sam's military camp. She bravely asked Sam to be just and use his wisdom instead of being angry and vengeful. She said that if Mehrab is the one to be blamed, it is okay to be angry with him, but the people of Kabul are innocent and have nothing to do with this matter. Sindukht looked at Sam and continued:

Mehrab has also prepared a strong army to defend Kabul, but we don't want any bloodshed over an issue that can be resolved through discussions.

Sam the Pahlawan (Hero) thought for a while and then accepted Sindukht's invitation for peace, thus ending the possibility of war between the two armies and peace prevailed.

SindukhBringin Gifts to Sam, from Fredousi'sShahnnama
15ᵗʰ century illustration

It is said that when the envious people mocked Sindokht for apologizing to Sam, Sindukht replied: "For me, the salvation of my people and my city is more important than my name and my treasures." It was then that the **name of Sindukht** remained as the savior of Kabul.

In Shahnama, Ferdausi also discusses Sindukht's daughter, "From Sindukht, a beautiful girl was born, named Rudaba of Kabul."

When she grew up, she was as brave and as wise as her mother. Zall, Sam's son, fell in love with her. Sindukht encouraged Rudaba to marry Zall, since he was a brave young man, and their marriage could end the animosity between the two families forever. Mehrab also agreed to their marriage on his wife's recommendation.

Rudaba married Zall, the brave son of Sam, the great Pahlawan; thus, the animosity between the two groups changed to friendship.

It is said that the wedding party of Rudaba was held at the Zarnegar Palace in Kabul, a name that has survived to this date. As a result of this marriage, Rustam was born, the most renowned legendary hero of Shahnamah, who has been compared to Hercules in Greek mythology.

The Story of TahminatheDaughter of King of Samangan

Years passed and Rustam grew as a mighty hero or Pahlawan. According to the myths in Shahnamah, one day Rustam traveled to Samangan. It is said that he came across Tahmina, the daughter of King of Samangan while searching for his fighting horse, Rakhsh. Firdausi describes the love story of Tahmina and Rustam as follows:

It was a beautiful sunny day in Samangan and Rustam decided to hunt. He hunted a number of deer and zebras. He lit a large fire in the forest and made a lot of kebabs from hunting meat. But he fell asleep after eating a big lunch. Firdausi adds: When Rustam was asleep, the thieves stole Rakhsh, his favorite horse. When Rustam woke up, he searched everywhere but did not find Rakhsh. So, with great sorrow and disappointment, he put the saddle of the horse on his shoulder and started to search for his horse. As he reached the gate of Samangan city, some people recognized him and informed the king of Samangan. When the ruler of Samangan learned of the arrival of that great hero in his town, he became very excited and arranged a lavish banquet for him. He kindly promised him that he would do his best to find the horse.

The night came, but there was no news of Rakhsh being found. Rustam was sad and disappointed, but when he was resting in despair on the bed in the guest house, a soft knock on the door caught his attention. And then he heard a soft delicate voice of a woman. Rustam looked at the door and saw a beautiful young woman standing in front of him. With an amazing charisma and beauty and a charming smile on her face, she welcomed him to her palace. Rustam looked at her with great astonishment, and the young girl started to talk. Firdausi describes this scene as follows:

I am Tahmina, the daughter of the king of Samangan
I am a swift chevalier and hunter
And tamer of leopards and lions
No one has ever seen my face in public
And no stranger has ever heard my voice
But I am here to help you since you are a famed hero
I give you my promises to find your horse

Fascinated by the beauty and kindness of the hospitable princess, the more Rustam heard from her, the more he fell in love with her. The next night, Rustam proposed to the King of Samangan to marry his daughter Tahmina, and the king gladly accepted. Tahmina's wisdom, purity, courage, and clean spirit made Rustam marry her. Tahmina's marriage to Rustam the Pahlawan, the famous hero, took place with great joy and participation of thousands of people of the historical city of Samangan.

Current view of Throne of Rustam in Samangan

According to the fables of the people of Samangan, the marriage of Rustam and Tahmina was held next to a large rock on a high hill, which is still called the Throne of Rustam.

As time passed, Tahmina gave birth to a healthy baby boy who was named Sohrab. Though, Rustam was always at war and in the absence of his father; Sohrab had to be raised by Tahmina. Sohrab became a great hero just like Rustam, but his story is a sad one; he was eventually killed by his father. The tragedy of Rustam and Sohrab became the topic of tragic fables in Eastern literature, especially in the epic fables of Shahnamah as the world became dark for Rustam when he learned that he had killed his own son unknowingly.

However, Rustam and Tahmina had a daughter named Gashsap who was later married to Gave legendary hero of Farah Province. (The present-day Jovian district of Farah Province is named after him). Like her mother, Gashsap was a brave woman. Gashsap was a skilled horse rider, excellent archer, and a swift sword fighter. According to Firdausi, no one could reach the level of her courage and fighting skills.

Although these epic stories do not have a very accurate historical feature, they do tell about the beliefs and viewpoint of the people of the land -- their courage, bravery, and skilled women of that era.

The Vedic and Avestan fables provide many examples of women personalities and their important roles in the society of that time. The most important of all was Anahita, the guardian angel of the Amu Darya (Oxus) and Helmand rivers.

She was also known as Naheed, the symbol of planet Venus. Old fables indicate that Zahak, a tyrant ruler, who apparently emerged from the mountains of Ghor, Afghanistan, attacked the kingdom of Yama, the most famous ruler of Balkh and defeated him. With Zahak's victory, a dark phase of cruelty ruled the Arian land. Many people were killed and Yama's daughters were imprisoned. However, Feraidoun, a legendary hero, rose to the occasion to fight Zahak. He had great reverence for Anahita and asked her for her assistance in the battle against Zahak. As a result of Anahita's blessings, he defeated Zahak.

Feraidoun's first noble act was to free the daughters of King Yama. The existence of Castle of Feraidoun in the province of Farah, the City of Zahak in Bamiyan, and the Medallion of Anahita found in Bagram near Kabul are ample physical evidence that this mythical episode did take place in the soil of Afghanistan and shows the importance of women in the ancient civilization of Ariana.

The Winged Gypsum Medallion of Anahita from Bagram,
circa First Century AD

The Historic Castle of Feraidoun, in Farah

References

Boyce, Mary (1975), "A History of Zoroastrianism", Vol. I, Leiden/Köln: Brill

Cumont, Franz (1926), "Anahita", in Hastings, James,

Encyclopedia of Religion and Ethics, Edinburgh

Habibi Abdul- Hai, "A Brief History of Afghanistan"1984

Kohzad Ahmad Ali, "History of Afghanistan" (Volume I), pre-Islamic era)

MacKenzie, David Neil (1964), "Zoroastrian Astrology in the 'Bundahišn'", Bulletin of the School of Oriental and African Studies, London: University of London

Mahmud Shah Mahmud - "Famous Women of Afghanistan" (Part 1)

Naweed Hamid," Art through the Ages in Afghanistan" Volume I 2011

CHAPTER TWO

Women of Ariana in the Greek Historical Texts

In the fifth century BC, during the golden age of Greek civilization, Herodotus founded the accurate style of recording historical events. He wrote about real people with specific names, places, and dates. As a result of his meticulous recording of events and developments, he is recognized as the father of existing history.

In addition to paying attention to Greece, Herodotus also wrote about the historical events and women of Eastern civilizations. In one of his notes, he mentions Queen Tomyris.

The Story of Queen Tomyris

Around 530 BC, Cyrus the Great Achaemenid king of Persia wanted to conquer the territory of the Sakas. Queen Tomyris was the ruler ofMassagetae tribe of the Sakas at that time. The residents of Sakas lived in northwest Afghanistan and parts of today's Turkmenistan. Queen Tomyris's husband had been dead for several years. Cyrus first proposed marriage to the widowed queen, but she refused, knowing that Cyrus's plan was to conquer her land. His proposal having been rejected; Cyrus sent an insulting message to the queen. Tymoris in return invited him to a battle to defend her dignity.

Cyrus' next step was to declare war. To win the war, the Persians played a trick. They knew that the Massagetae people were not accustomed to drinking wine, so they placed large amounts of wine musk in their camp at night. A secret agent of Cyrus came to Sakas and encouraged them to drink the wine. He convinced the queen's soldiers to drink the refreshing liquid, which gave Cyrus the upper hand and allowed him to defeat his enemies with little effort. During the battle, a Sakas general and the queen's young son were captured. Queen Tomyris was outraged to hear this shocking news especially that of her son's capture. Being the determined and brave queen that she was, Tomyris sent the following message to Cyrus:

You, Cyrus, whose thirst for bloodshed never ends, do not rejoice in what you have done. When wine enters your body, you say evil words; if you have won the war by deceiving my son, don't be proud, because you are not a true warrior. Now, take a good word of advice: Return my son to me and leave this country for your own safety. A third of my forces have not yet fought. If you do not do this, I swear to the Sun that I will shed your blood.

Sadly, the queen's son was ultimately killed in the Persian camp. In retaliation, she ordered the Sakas soldiers to attack Cyrus' camp and kill all the Persians. The next morning, the victorious queen went to search for Cyrus' body among the dead. She eventually found the lifeless body of Cyrus and ordered her soldiers to cut his head and plunge it into a sack filled with blood and said: "I am now sending your beheaded body to your country so that no one from your country ever attempts to invade my land."

Death of Cyrus the Great, by Peter Pall Rubens

Herodotus adds, "Many stories have been told about the death of Cyrus, but what I have said is the most credible." Over time, his narrative took hold and became a popular topic in the literature, paintings, and plays of the Renaissance period. Peter Paul Rubens, the famous Dutch artist, even depicted this scene in a painting of striking classical style.

Women of Ariana in Alexander's Companions' Writings

In 328 BC, Alexander, son of Philip, king of Macedonia, who was known as the greatest conqueror of the ancient world, launched his first campaign in Afghanistan. As a young prince, Alexander was a student of Aristotle, one of the most renowned Greek philosophers in the 4th century BC. Upon Aristotle's advice, he asked a number of historians to accompany him in his battles and take detailed notes as he embarked on his invasions and conquests.

Following Alexander's guidance, Greek historians and scholars continued to record the cultural events and developments as they explored the newly discovered civilization of Eastern countries, especially the land of Ariana. After the defeat of the Persians, Alexander attacked Aria (Herat), and later Arachosia (Kandahar), and Kabul to reach Bactria. It took him five years battaling the people of Ariana (today's Afghanistan) without having a major success. His soldiers faced severe resistance and challenges in the process Alexander lost his best soldiers without achieving any significant victory. Olympias, Alexander's mother, eventually sent him a note inquiring about his health and the reasons for his failed military campaigns in Ariana. According to Greek historians, Alexander's response to his mother was:

"I am engaged in battle in the land of lions, where at every step brave warrior meets my soldiers like a wall of steel. Mother! You have given birth to only one Alexander, but every mother in this land has given birth to an Alexander. "

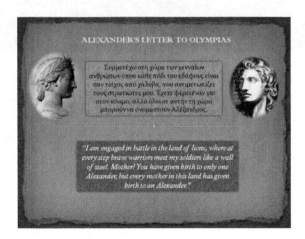

The Story of Roxana

When he finally reached Bactria, Alexander's soldiers shot arrows, stones, and fire with catapults at Bactrian's stronghold, but continued to have little success.

One early morning, a tired and frustrated Alexander was surprised by the sight of a beautiful, young Bactrian girl approaching him. He looked at her with awe as the young girl said that her name was Roxana, and she had come to see him in person to ask some questions.

She had many questions for him: "Why don't you talk to us like a civilized person instead of shooting fire and arrows at us? What is the cause of your anger and selfishness? What is the reason for this bloody war anyway? We have not attacked your country or burned your cities. Please answer me. I want to know."

Alexander the Great Meeting Roxane,
Pietro Antonio Rotari (1756), Hermitage Museum, Saint Petersburg, Russia

It is said that Alexander remained silent as he didn't have a logical answer to Roxana's meaningful and honest questions. She fascinated him with her

17

dignity, intelligence, and beauty. When she left, some of Alexander's companions advised him that he should make peace with the Bactrians and propose marriage to Roxana, so that Greeks and Bactrian could live in peace and have friendly relationships.

Wedding Ceremony of Alexander and Roxana

A number of Alexander's generals feared that the Greek Army might gradually vanish in the harsh environment of Hindu-Kush Mountains and die from fatigue and hunger. However, some of his arrogant generals opposed the idea. A few days later, Alexander made his decision and proposed marriage to Roxana by talking to Oxyartes, Roxana's father. Hokhyar Khan (*Oxyartes in Greek*) agreed and their marriage took place at the foothills of the high mountains of Hindu Kush. According to Callisthenes of Olynthus, Alexander's historian, Alexander's marriage to Roxana was in fact the marriage of two cultures. The people of Bactria accepted Alexander as their son-in-law, and the Greeks in turn mingled with the Bactrians in a peaceful ambiance. A few months passed, and then Alexander decided to conquer India with the help of Arian people. While in India, he fell ill due to malaria and, upon his mother's request, decided to return to his country. On the way to Greece, he spent some time in Babylon, present-day Iraq, and then married Barsina, the daughter of the late king of Persia Darius the 3rd.

Due to the region's hot and humid climate, which was not suitable for his health, Alexander eventually died in Babylon at the age of 32, leaving behind a vast empire and estate without a successor.

After his death, Alexander's generals decided to divide his great empire among them. At this time, Roxana had just given birth to her son, Alexander IV. The people of Bakhtar expected Roxana to proclaim Alexander IV as king and for her to assume power as the mother of the crown prince. While in the city of Susa in Persia, Roxana decided to travel to Babylon to negotiate with Alexander's generals and claim her son's rights to the crown. As the queen mother, she sought to independently rule Bacteria, her homeland. But when she arrived in Babylon, Alexander's powerful generals imprisoned her for being allegedly involved in the recent murder of Barsina, who was mysteriously killed in a horrible dungeon while still carrying Alexander's child in her womb.

Olampias's Memories of Alexander's Childhood during His Introduction to Aristotle
Artist: Gerard Hoet Augusta, Stylianou Art Collections

19

A desperate Roxana then wrote a letter to Olympias, Alexander's mother, asking her for help. Roxana's letter reminded Olympias of her own son's childhood and evoked motherly love in her heart for the safety of her grandson. Knowing thatRoxana was innocent, she firmly ordered his generals to release Roxana and her son from the prison of Babylon and bring them to Greece. With great difficulty and the help of her queen's loyal soldiers, Roxana was finally released and returned to Greece. She spent eleven years with Olympias in Greece. When Alexander IV reached the age of eleven, Olympias decided to crown him as the only legitimate Crown Prince of Alexander's Empire.

The news spread quickly among those who had their eyes on the throne of Alexander's vast empire, and it was then that one of Alexander's greedy generals, Cassander, attacked the queen's palace and killed Olympias, Roxana, and the young crown prince. Referred to as a tragic tale in classical European literature, the story of Roxana ended sadly.

With the spread of this news, the people of Bakhtar (Bactria) revolted. Euthydemus, one of Alexander's loyal and devoted generals living in Bactria, united the people of Bactria and declared the Greco-Bactrian independent government. But people remembered Roxana's exciting life story, and she became the symbol of justice for centuries to come.

Archeologists have recently unearthed a magnificent tomb in the ancient Greek city of Amphipolis in northern Greece. It is believed to belong to Roxana and her son. Its construction method is different from the classical Greek architectural style, containing features of Bactrian architecture, especially in its stonework and capitals. It is quite possible that some of Roxana's relatives may have gone to Greece with a group of Bactrian architects to build the tomb of Roxana and her son. Cassander hid the burial place of Alexander's mother, son, and his wife during his reign. Perhaps for this reason, their tomb was built shortly after their death.

Women of Ancient Bactria

Bactria or ancient Balkh of Ariana was the center of Eastern civilization in the 3rd century BC. During this era, Greek culture mixed with the ancient civilization of Ariana. Eucratides, King of Bactria, founded the city of Eucratideia or today's Ai Khanum. The city of Ai Khanum, meaning the Moon Lady, is located in Takhar province, near Oxus and Kokcha rivers. Archeologists have discovered artwork of very advanced civilizations of the distant past in the ancient city of Ai Khanum. Among the many beautiful pieces of artwork found in Ai Khanum is a silver plate decorated with gold, known as the famous Cybele Plate. It depicts the natural power of the Goddess Cybele and the importance of women during that period. (Cybele is a Greek name for the Eastern goddess of mountains, MATAR KUBILEYA.)

Cybele Plate & Portrait of a Bactrian Lady from Ai Khanum, 3rd century BC.

MatarKubileya was the guardian angel of nature, especially of the mountains in the Eastern culture. Her golden chariot was driven by two lions. This goddess was highly respected in most parts of Asia, ranging from Asia Minor (Turkey) to Kabul. Later, the Romans also began to believe in her, which prompted the spread of her statues all over Europe.

The Cybele Plate discovered from Ai Khanum is the oldest manifestation of the Goddess Cybele in the ancient world. The lions that pull her chariot represent her authority over nature. This fable states the fact that even lions, nature's strongest animals, surrender to Mother Kubileya. This ancient silver plate unearthed from Ai Khanum attests to the high status of mother in Bactrian culture. Similarly, the marble statue of the Bactrian Lady, depicting an Oriental woman, shows the importance of women in Greco- Bactrian civilization.

Amazingly, several statues of Athena, the Greek goddess of wisdom, uncovered by the French Archeological Teem, (DAFA) from Bagram also signifies the general respect of the people of Ariana for female characters. Similarly, the statues of Adina, the mother goddess in eastern cultures, demonstrate the strong personality, courage, bravery, and respect of women in the Afghan society during this timeframe.

Women in Afghanistan enjoyed a very high status during the Sakas and Koshan civilizations. The most important historical treasures of Afghanistan, made of pure gold, were found in Sheberghan (Tella Tapa) or the Golden Mound, mostly belonging to influential women.

Examples of Women Jewelry from the Gold Treasures of Afghanistan

Among the six graves that have been discovered from the royal graveyard of Sheberghan, only one tomb is of a male king; the rest belong to women. Thus, it is fair to conclude that powerful women ruled in this area one after another and enjoyed great power and wealth. The ornaments of these powerful princesses and queens, in addition to being created with a special taste, tell popular fables. The gold treasure of Sheberghan was created based on the women's taste and is the second valuable golden horde after the treasures of the Egyptian pharaohs.

Status of Women in the Koshanian Era

Nana, the mother goddess, was an important and popular dietyduring the Koshanian period. She was highly respected during this era.

At the beginning of the Second century AD, Emperor Kanishka, the powerful ruler of Ariana, built a large temple in her honor, called the *Temple of "Nana*," meaning "Mother Goddess". This ancient temple is located in the present-day Baghlan Province. In this grand temple, a historical stone tablet has been discovered that describesthe importance and high status of a mother during this era.

The lion under Nana's knee signifies that all the brave warriors should first honor their mothers and then claim the title of bravery. During the Koshanian period, the word mother conveyed the concept of a savior and a rescuer

Statue of the Mother Goddess, Nana, Gandaharan School of Art

who provided a sanctuary to those in need of protection. The term "motherland" in Afghan culture still expresses this concept, that is, to have the highest reverence for mothers and country.

In southern Afghanistan, from Kunar and Nangarhar to Kandahar and Helmand, women continue to this day to play an important role in resolving disputes and achieving peaceful and harmonious relations among families and communities. For example, if an elderly lady enters a tense atmosphere between two quarreling groups and puts a rock on the ground to end the conflict, both sides will stop fighting out of respect for the dignity of the elderly lady.

This ancient custom is mentioned in the Pashto language as Tiga, which means stone. This tradition is still honored in some villages of Afghanistan. The tradition of Nanawati was also performed by women to bring peace and stop a possible bloodshed by throwing her shawl on the ground to stop the confrontation. Usually, both sides would stop fighting in honor of the woman who has come to represent Nanawati. These traditions still exist in parts of Afghanistan.

As demonstrated by these stories, statues, paintings, and ancient literature, it is fair to say that from the beginning of the life of early humans to the Koshanian era and later periods, women played significant roles in society. During this era, women played their vital roles with courage, moderation, and sacrifice while leaving their mark in history. While most of these women are real figures and a few are legendary and mythical figures, all testify to the importance of women and their constructive roles in ancient Afghanistan.Moreover, numerous statues of women from the Koshan period clearly demonstrate the social status, lifestyle, costumes and hairstyle of these women in various pre-Islamic periods.

Portraits of Women from Koshanian Period,
Temple of Hadda, Jalalabad 2nd to 3rd century AD

The Bravery of a Young Kabul Woman

The ancient people of Kabul had a tyrant king named Zanburak Shah in the beginning of 7th century AD. One day, he decided to build a wall on theAsmayee-and Shirt DarwazaMountains, located in the heart of the city. His goal was to protect and defend Kabul from invading armies. He hired many workers to build the wall. Cruel and uncaring, his officers would force the workers to work harder beyond their capacity, and whenever workers needed to rest, the king's soldiers would whip them and sometimes put them in the wall in place of bricks.

Learning about the mistreatment and cruelty of the king and his officers, a young girl, fed up with the brutality of the Zanburak Shah, took it upon herself to do something about this tyrant. It is said that her young fiancé was among the workers who was not receiving any compensation for his work, which he needed for their upcoming wedding. Further, he was not allowed to take time off from work. So, his fiancée decided to free the people of Kabul from this tyrant for once and for all. Pretending to be just like another laborer, she started the day like the rest of the workers. But one day, when the king was watching the progress of the project, the young girl covered her face from him. The king asked in surprise, "Why do you cover your face from me when you do not cover your face from other men?"

The girl replied, "Because they are women just like me, and they do not have the guts to defend their rights against an oppressive king like you. But I am a brave woman, and I will not allow anyone to commit such atrocities against me and the people of Kabul." While she was shouting at him, she managed to hurl a rock at his head with great force, causing him to drop to the ground. Having witnessed the courage of this young woman, the workers revolted, resulting in an uprising and the demise of the king. Although the name of this young girl is not mentioned in history books, there have been different narrations of this incident attesting to her heroism and bravery. Afghan history books are filled with many examples of such heroic women.

A View of Kabul Walls on the Mountaintop

References:

An Historical Guide to Afghanistan by Nancy H. Dupree, Afghanistan Tourist Org. Kabul, 1972

A Concise History of Afghanistan, By A. Habibi, Kabul Afghanistan, 1965

Art through the Ages in Afghanistan by Hamid Naweed, 2014

History of Afghanistan by Ahmad Ali Kohzad

Deeds of Alexander by Callisthenes (the official historian)

Frank W. Walbank, the Editors of Encyclopaedia Britannica

History of Alexander "Cleitarchus". Encyclopædia Britannica.

Vol. 6, Cambridge University Press.

Work of Ephippus of Olynthus, the Oxford Classical Dictionary

Carney, Elizabeth Donnelly (1996), "Alexander and Persian Women"

The American Journal of Philology,

Simpson, William (1881). "Art. VII. / On the Identification of Nagarahara, with reference to the Travels of Hiouen-Thsang". Journal of the Royal Asiatic Society

Olympias, the Mighty Mother of Alexander the Great". National Geographic Society. 2019.

Waterfield, Robin (2011). Dividing the Spoils: The War for Alexander the Great's Empire. New York: Oxford University Press.

CHAPTER THREE

Afghan Women in the Beginning of Islamic Era

With the emergence of Islam in the middle of the seventh century AD, great changes took place in all social relationships, beliefs, customs, traditions, way of thinking, and even the calligraphy of Eastern countries.

In the early days of Islam, women's status and prestige was substantially elevated during the lifetime of the Prophet, as well as during the era of Rashidun Caliphs (the Righteous Caliphs). The women played prominent roles in the social life of the city of Medina, whose people had just converted to Islam.

The women of Medina and then Mecca had their own social status and freedoms in accordance to Islamic law. To this date, Islamic traditions and beliefs attribute the highest status to a mother. Prophet Mohammed (PBUH) has even said that Heaven lies under the feet of our mothers, thus, giving mothers the highest honor and status in society. During this timeframe, women frequently met with the Prophet and asked for his guidance and advice in various matters of life.

However, after the reign of Rashidun Caliphs, followed by the emergence of Umayyad and then Abbasid Caliphs, Islamic societies slowly underwent many changes in terms of political, administrative, and ideological views. Thus, the role of women in the 8th and 9th century AD gradually changed, losing its prominence to male dominance. Historians of this era have spoken less about women although there have been a few written articles about women of fame during this period.

This section, however, deals with the life stories of the few well-known women who lived in Afghanistan during this period.

The Legend of Bibi Hoor and Bibi Noor

Among the famous women of this period, whose names are mentioned in historical documents, are the two famous sisters, named Bibi Hoor and Bibi Noor. According to Mir Khond, prominent historian of the 15th century in Herat, Bibi Hoor and Bibi Noor lived in the distant past, around the 8th century AD. But some people think that they lived in pre-Islamic times much before the 8th century. The people of Herat

27

believed that the two sisters were kind and benevolent. The construction of the Malan Bridge was very beneficial for the merchants and inhabitants of Herat. During this time the city of Herat had four grand gates important for commerce. The Malan Bridge was built over Harirud River. It was located to the south of Kandahar Gate, where the caravans of goods coming from the north were traveling from Herat to Kandahar and subsequently to the Indian subcontinent. The construction of this majestic bridge is credited to Bibi Hoor and Bibi Noor, since they played a valuable role in building this grand historical bridge.

A View of Malan Historical Bridge, Herat, Afghanistan

According to Nancy Hatch Dupree, the two benevolent sisters had a green farm next to Hari-Rud River. Their farm housed a large poultry farm and a charming stream. Bibi Hoor and Bibi Noor recognized the daily challenges of the ordinary people and trade caravans crossing the Hari-Rod River, especially during the rainy and snowy seasons when their challenges of crossing the river were doubled. The two caring sisters decided to build a bridge that could connect the villages on the two opposite banks of the river. They reached out the residents of their own villages and other nearby villages, located on the banks of the river and shared their idea with the merchants and caravan owners. Thus began the start of their fundraising and the eventual construction of the bridge. Since both sisters were trustworthy, honest, and wealthy landowners, the people of Herat entrusted to them the construction of the project. Soon, Bibi Hoor and Bibi Noor raised large sums of money by encouraging the wealthy people of Herat to build the bridge. It is said that they also suggested that the mud for making the bricks should be mixed with egg yolk so the bricks can withstand the strong waves of Hari Rod River. Bibi Hoor and Bibi Noor donated large portions of their own farms and collected eggs from other farm owners. After a while, with the hard work and perseverance of the people of Malan village and obviously the courage of the two benevolent sisters, a large bridge was built, which is one of the longest historical bridges in Afghanistan. The Malan Bridge has nineteen porticos, and it is still in use after nearly a thousand years. Mir-Khond, the famous historian of the Timurid era adds:

When Shahrokh Mirza, the great Sultan of Herat learned of this story, he sent his men to the burial of Bibi Hour and Bibi Noor and ordered them to build a dome over their tombs.

The tomb of Bibi Hour and Bibi Noor is located in the old city of Herat. On Wednesdays, people still visit their tomb to pay their respects. The account of these two brave sisters is also mentioned in the historical notes of Sultan Abu Saeed Era.

However, the construction of this bridge has also been attributed to several other legendary figures and dynasties. The people of Herat link the construction of Malan Bridge to another historical fable, the love story of "Zohra and Feraidoun." A popular folk song narrates the love story of Zohra and Feraidoun and how they met each other on this legendary bridge, and attributes its construction to Feraidoun's father in Zoroastrian time. There are several accounts regarding the construction date of Malan Bridge, and its construction is also attributed to the reign of Seljuks.

During the 7th and 8th centuries AD, many political and social changes occurred in Islamic countries and more historical accounts were written by Arab and non-Arab historians about the Eastern countries.

During this time, the Medieval Khurasan, which covered most of the territory of today's Afghanistan, was a rich land with very advanced culture. The Arabs referred to it as the land of poetry and the Rising Sun.

Many prominent and distinguished women left their mark in the history of this ancient land. The following section deals with the activities and life histories of the women whose names are recorded in historical documents.

Margile Herawi

One of the famous women of Khurasan or today's Afghanistan during the 8th century is a brave woman named Margile (also spelled as Marjila by Arab historians), whose life was full of ups and downs as well as charms. She was the daughter of Sies Herawi, a freedom fighter known as Master Sies among the people of Herat. Master Sies spoke eloquently and was a famous speaker for the independence of Khurasan from the control of Abbasid Caliphs of Baghdad. He was the leader of the White Flag Movement in Herat. The movement started against the Baghdad Caliphs after the cowardly killing of Abu Muslim Khorasani by Abu al-AbassSafah, the tyrant caliph who carried Black flags.

Marjila participated in all of the speeches of her father against the tyranny of Al-Mehdi, the Caliph of Baghdad. When Harun al-Rashid, his successor became the leader of Baghdad, Sies was still encouraging people to fight for their independence from the Abbasid Caliphs while Marjila was her father's faithful follower. Arab historians have described Marjila as a tall, brave, woman with a darker complexion. She was fighting side by side with her father when Harun Al-Rashid attacked Herat in an attempt to capture Sites. But Sies and his daughter along with their followers took refuge in the mountains on the outskirts of the city of Herat, and established their resistance camp in a remote mountainous spot.

However, the spies of Harun al-Rashid revealed their center of resistance to the caliph, and it was then that Harun al-Rashid's best soldiers ambushed their base, killed all their followers but kept the father and daughter alive for public punishment in Baghdad. Sies was imprisoned and later killed in the prison. The caliph instructed that Marjila be part of his harem and work for his wife, Zubaida Khatun, as a personal maid. Despite the fact that Marjila was deeply distressed and disappointed by the death of her father, she never lost her pride and self-esteem until she was forcibly impregnated by Harun Al-Rashid. She gave birth to Mamun Al-Rashid, the most powerful ruler in the Abbasid Dynasty. Marjila raised her son with the ornament of knowledge and human feeling, passing on to him the knowledge and wisdom she had acquired from her father. Mamun also learned all fighting skills from the best generals in his father's army. Consequently, he became a man with superior warfare skills and general knowledge compared to his brother, Amin al-Rashid, Queen Zubaida's son. Historians write that Amin was a man of luxury and comfort. While Amin was very irresponsible, Mamun showed much better leadership skills, determination, decisiveness, and responsibility.

Many historians, including Al-Tabari, have written that Mamun became the governor of Khurasan. Marjila entered the city of her father where she was born and had lost her loved ones. She asked her son to do his best in developing the city of Herat and focus on the public welfare of her hometown.

Chaliph Mamoon Al-Rasid, the Brrve Son of Margile Herawi

After the death of Harun al-Rashid, Amin, who was his crown prince, took the throne of the caliphate, but due to his poor leadership, people were not happy. He blamed his brother and ordered Mamun's arrest. Mamun did not accept his unjust decision. Amin sent an army to Herat for his capture, but Mamun resisted and with the help of Tahir, a brave general from Fushnj of Herat, defeated Amin's forces.

Mamun became the sole ruler of Baghdad. It is said that Marjila, as the Queen Mother, earned great respect and authority as a result. She became the source of many services in Iraq, Syria, Persia and Khurasan.

This is the story of Marjila, a brave young woman who was taken captive, became a slave girl, and then with great self-confidence and firm belief in justice, became the most powerful queen of the Islamic world.

Khadija of Sarakhs

According to Arab historians, when Marjila came to Herat, she was looking for a beautiful, educated young girl worthy of marrying Mamun al-Rashid, her son. She had to be caring, smart, and come from a highly educated and well-respected family background to be the wife of the caliph. A young poetess named Khadija from Herat, famous for her poetic talent and knowledge, was deemed a good match for her son.

Khadija was the daughter of Hassan bin Sahl from Sarakhs, located in the north of Herat on the border of present-day Turkmenistan and Iran. Back then, it was considered part of the Herat municipality.

Marjila met a very talented young lady who later became Queen of Mamun al-Rashid.

Towards the beginning the 9th century AD, Khadija went to Baghdad with Mamun Al Rashid, learned the Arabic language fluently, and subsequently composed eloquent poems in Arabic. Khadija's Arabic poems have been published in *"The Movement of Women in Poetry and Literature"* by the Egyptian scholar Al-Suyuti, as well as in various documents in Cairo. According to Arab historians, when Mamun al-Rashid passed away in Baghdad, Khadija wrote a very eloquent, emotional, and moving eulogy.

During the caliphate of Mamun al-Rashid, the first independent government in present-day Afghanistan was established in the city of Herat by Tahir Fushnji. At that time, Herat was the center of theTahirid Dynasty and a commercial city. The metalworking industry of this era was superb and the goldsmiths of Herat created the most exquisite jewelry and crockery. Of course, the taste of women played an important role in the creation of these fine artifacts.

The Beatiful Metalwork of Herat from Medieval Times

32

Ratiba Herawi

Ratiba Herawi lived in the first half of the 9th century AD during the reign of Tahir ibn Abdullah, the last king of Tahirid dynasty. Ratiba was a talented poetess and musician. Everyone admired her, and she was famous in that crowded city of Herat. According to the famous medieval time historian, Minhaj Siraj Jawzjani, she was very beautiful and had a mesmerizing voice. She sang mostly romantic lyrics and played the harp. She was so beautiful that Tahir bin Abdullah, the wealthy monarch of Khurasan, fell in love with her. But at that time, a man named Mahmud Waraq from Nishapur bought Ratiba from her master and took her to Neyshabur. The king sent an envoy to Mahmud Waraq and offered a large sum of gold in exchange for her. But Mahmud's response was, "Oh dear King, I will give you all my wealth, but not Ratiba."

The king's envoy asking for the return of Ratiba

It is said that since Ratiba spent the rest of her life in Nishapur, she is also known as Neyshaburi, but there is no record of her poems.

References

Hugh N. Kennedy, the Early Abbasid Caliphate, a political History,
Croom Helm, London, 1981

Bosworth, C. E. (1969). "The Ṭāhirids and Persian Literature

Nancy H. Dupree, "A Historical Guide to Afghanistan"

Mir Gholam M Ghobar "Afghanistan In The Course Of History Vol.2 in English

Professor A. Habibi, "A Concise History of Afghanistan"

Encyclopaedia of Islam, New Edition, Volume VI: Mahk–Mid. Leiden: E. J. Brill. pp. 331–339

Bosworth, C. E., ed. (1989). The History of al-Ṭabarī, Volume XXX: The 'Abbāsid Caliphate in Equilibrium: The Caliphates of Mūsā al-Hādī and Hārūn al-Rashīd, A.D. 785–809/A.H. 169–192. SUNY Series in Near Eastern Studies. Albany, New York: State University of New York Press

Abbott, Nabia (1946). Two Queens of Baghdad: Mother and Wife of Hārūn Al Rashīd. University of Chicago Press.

CHAPTER FOUR

Women of the Saffarid, Samanid and
Al-Ferighun Dynasties (861 to 1003 AD)

The powerful Saffarid Kingdom was founded by Ya'qub Laith Saffar in the ancient city of Zaranj, in Southwest Afghanistan on the bank of the Helmand River, around 861 AD. Ya'qub was a brave young man from among the commoners of Zaranj whose father was a coppersmith. He stood up against the cruelties and unjust behavior of the Arab Governor of Zaranj. Yaqub was supported by a group of philanthropic women who lived in the city of Zaranj; they were referred to as the ladies of compassion and kindness. They all stood firmly behind Ya'qub and his brave knights, called the Ayyars and supported him for his struggles against the Abbasid Caliphs who meddled in these ladies' homeland.

These good women were the mothers, wives, sisters, and family members of influential rulers who believed in fairness and kindness. Apparently, they were the survivors of kingGashtasp of Balkh who had settled in Zaranj in the pre-Islamic times. Their ancestors were once the keepers of the Fire Temple of the city, but by the 8th century AD, they had all become devout Muslims.

When Hassan Basri, one of the greatest scholars of Islam, came to Sistan and Farah, many people converted to Islam and decided to build a mosque to worship Almighty God. This was the very first mosque which was ever built in Afghanistan. Toward the construction of the mosque, the influential ladies of Farah and Zaranj made generous donations, which even included all their jewelry and large sums of money to make Adina Mosque a reality. The mosque was called Adina, which means Friday in Dari.

The History of Sistan (author unknown) describes the Adina Mosque as very charming, with a large pool in its courtyard surrounded by a pleasant garden irrigated by a canal from the Helmand River. Arab historians refer to the downtown part of Zaranj as a city with a very beautiful view.

The "kind and compassionate" ladies of Zaranj showed great goodwill and affection to the mystics and Sufis and also provided much help to the poor and needy of the city. With their assistance, Ya'qub Laith Saffar soon became the powerful king of

Zaranj. He had a great deal of respect for these women and assigned his knights to protect them. In the history books of Sistan, it is mentioned that one of Ya'qub Laith Saffarid'ssons married the daughter of Afifa Malek Banu, an influential lady from the Kindness Dynasty (MolukMehrabani in Farsi). Historical documents show that the descendents of MolukMehrabani, the Kind Rulers, lived honorable lives in Nimroz Province of Afghanistan until the time of Ahmad Shah Durrani, whose wife was from this prestigious and hospitable family.

In addition to the women of the Kindness Rulers, another dynasty, known as the Kings of Nasr, also lived in the southwestern part of Afghanistan, namely the regions of Farah, Nimroz and Helmand. The women of this dynasty also believed in helping the poor and the needy. They built homes for the disadvantaged and guest houses for needy travelers. Most of these kind women devoted their capital to helping the poor.

The Remains of Adina Mosque in the City of Zaranj

Famous Women of the Samanid Period

The Samanid dynasty came to power immediately after the fall of the Saffarids toward the end of the 9th century AD. The Samanid kings were originally from the Saman village of Balkh, the base of their power. In the Samanid era, poetry and literature developed significantly. Great poets, scholars and intellectuals emerged who laid the foundations of Dari literature and the style of poetry writing which was special to Khurasan. The pillars of this intellectual movement were Shahid Balkhi, Abu-Shkour Balkhi, Ibn-Sina of Balkh (Avicenna in English), Daqiqi Balkhi, Rabia Balkhi and RudakiSamarkandi from Samarkand. Their remarkable work is a testament to the cultural achievements of this period.

The economic growth during this period is attributed to the significant contributions of a powerful group of people called the clan of Ferighun. They lived in northern Afghanistan in Jawzjan, Sar-e-Pul, parts of Balkh and Faryab with influence extending from Badakhshan to Ghore and Ghazni. The Ferighunid men were the breeders of the best breed of horses, and the women of this distinguished clan made the most beautiful carpets and rugs in the region. Professor Habibi has addressed them as people of peace, poetry, and business. Ferighunid people played a major role in the economic growth of the country, benefitting the Samanid Empire.

The Ladies of Kandrum

During this period, the ancient Silk Road was still connecting China to Islamic World and Byzantine, the (Eastern Roman Empire.) According to the author of "Hudud al-Alam" (The Limits of the World), the city of Kandrum in today's Anbar or Sar-e-Pul, Afghanistan was a wealthy and prosperous town.

The ladies of Kandrum were famous for carpet weaving, wool industry, fine silk garment making, embroidery, and precious, decorative tapestries with animal and bird motifs.

An illustration of a Kundram Lady

It is said that there was a very active and smart business lady known as Kandrum Khatun. She had become very rich as a result of recruiting and training the most talented carpet weavers and tailors in the region. She had partnered and established profitable business relationships with women of Faryab, Jawzijan,

Balkh and Merv. The women of this region are still famous for making beautiful carpets, rugs, and garments with the finest embroidery.

Women Costum from Northern Afghanistan

The anonymous author of the book "Hudud al-Alam" also describes the province of today's Jawzjan as a rich and prosperous area during the rule of the Samanids and the rule of Al-Ferighun. The book makes reference to the existence of gold, silver, lead and coal in the area. The traders who were traveling from China to Khwarizm often passed through Jawzjan. During this time, Herat was also a flourishing business center. It had a large market to accommodate ladies to display and sell their fine products, especially their world-renowned tapestries.

The Copenhagen Museum in Denmark and several personal galleries in Europe still have examples of these thousand- year old fine products.

The tapestry adorned with the images of two oxen is most probably created by women. This historic tapestry which is on display in the Copenhagen Museum shows the 9th century's women artistic talent.

Throughout this time, women were active in all aspects of life, including business and making fine handicrafts, but all their activities were not limited to making beautiful rugs and pottery; among them, there were also many talented writers, educators, and poets.

Tapestary and Pottery of the Samanid Era 9th century AD

Rabia Balkhi

During the rule of the Samanids, Dari literature reached its peak and Rabia, the daughter of the ruler of Balkh, known as Rabia Balkhi, was the very first poetess of this era.

Rabia was the daughter of Ka'bQazdari, the powerful governor of Balkh. Rabia's

family had migrated from Zaranj to Balkh, where she was raised. Not much is known about Rabia's childhood, but when she began composing poetry as a young talented lady, her father, who was a highly educated and knowledgeable person, gave her his full support so that she could receive the best education in the field of literature, history, philosophy, theology and sciences. From her poems, one can easily conclude that she had received excellent education from the best teachers of that time.

There is much written about Rabia's literary talent and her ability in composing fine poetry. Her poems express her honest feelings and the events of her life.

Prominent scholars and poets such as Attar Neyshapouri and AbdurahmanJaami, the great poet of Herat, have described Rabia Balkhi as a very gifted and talented young lady and have praised her poems as most moving and romantic. Her poems tell us that she was in love with Baktash, a strong hansome military officer, who was a slave of her father. The romantic love story of a beautiful princess with a slave is a popular topic that many writers have written about. And, Attar Neyshapour, too, makes reference to a secret letter sent by Rabia to Baktash with the aid of her maid. According to Neyshapouri, this letter was accompanied by love poems, and Attar adds that Rabia's love for Baktash was a divine love, away from physical love, as he analyzes her poem on the topic of love.

The Ocean of Love

When I first felt his love in my heart
I tried hard not to fall in love, but to no avail
Love is like a boundless ocean
And I am an inexperienced swimmer
To reach true love
One must like the unpleasant
View the ugly as beauty
And take poison as honey
I tried to be this untamed love stallion
But I discovered its reins too suffocating around my neck
Not knowing that its reigns would be so suffocating

Although this poem shows Rabia's interest in Baktash, in reality Rabia explains the main nature of love, especially when she talks about the sea of love that has no boundaries. Since Attar sees man as being inherently a creature bound by time and space, he describes Rabia's love as something divine, expressing the unlimited love that Almighty God has created in our hearts.

In addition to the excellent education that she received as was recommended by her father, this young, smart princess spent most of her time reading the books of the most renowned scholars of the time. Rabia lived in the golden age of Balkh in the 9th century AD. It is said that Rabia herself was interested in teaching what she learned from the great thinkers to other women and girls who did not have similar opportunities for learning as Rabia did. She organized literary gatherings for the young girls and women who were interested in learning poetry and other fields of knowledge.

Rabia was also fascinated by the art of painting. In the poem below, she creates literary images and discusses Mani, the famous painter of ancient times whose book, Arjang, is full of colorful paintings.

The Garden (An Allegorical Poem)

The flower beds that live in the garden
Remind us of Mani's Paintings
The beautiful roses may have taken their charm from
Lily's face, or from the shining goblet of tulips
The narcissus flowers have golden caps
Have they borrowed them from the King's crown?
The violet looks like monks in their blue robes
Perhaps they don't fear to change their religion

Ka'b appointed Baktash, one of his loyal slaves, to teach Rabia all fighting techniques and cavalry. It is said that after a while, Rabia, in shooting arrows and horse riding, surpassed even her personal faithful trainer, Baktash himself. Baktash was always in Rabia's service ordered by Amir. Memorable days passed and they fell in love with each other. But due to his respect for the Ka'b family, Baktash did not express his feelings openly to Rabia.

It is said that one day Rabia's father sent Baktash to war as chief of the army. It was not too long before the news of Baktash's wounded state reached Rabia. She bravely wore armor and a mask and rushed to the battlefield to rescue Baktash. She stopped the opposing army with her arrows and saved Baktash's life. It was then that she realized how important he was in her life.

However, Ka'b, Rabia's father, who considered his daughter to be one of the most important women in society, advised her to be careful in her behavior and speech with Baktash and not to get too close to him. But Rabia's love for Baktash grew more and stronger every day.

On the other hand, Baktash, who had great respect for Amir Ka'b, understood his reasonable concern and out of respect, stayed away from Rabia. But Rabia, who could not bear the distant from Baktash, wrote this poem:

My invitation to you is to fall in love
With a heartbreaking person just like yourself
So, you can experience the pain of love,
Fall in anguish, and understand my feelings

Some time passed and eventually Ka'b departed from this world. He was replaced by Harith, Rabia's brother, who had been jealous of his sister from a young age. He began his rule with cruelty and meanness. His first goal was to keep Baktash away from Balkh and to limit Rabia's interactions with him. She was not even allowed to leave the palace.

One night Harith was invited by the king of Bukhara, and Rudaki, the old poet from Samarkand, who had lost his sight, was also among the guests. During the pleasant royal party, Rudaki was asked to play his harp and sing. Everyone was absorbed by Rudaki's superb performance. During his recital, Rudaki sang one of Rabia's poems. Not noticing that Harith, Rabia's fanatical brother, was among the guests, he said that these poems were written by Rabia, the daughter of Amir Ka'b for her great love to Baktash, the slave of his family.

Hearing this, Harith became very angry, biting his lips, and left the party. With extreme anger, he hurried to Balkh to punish his sister.

When he reached his palace, Harith shouted frantically that Rabia must be taken to the dungeon and be killed in an underground bath. He ordered that her blood vessels must be cut to effect slow, gradual, painful death. The executioners cut Rabia's blood vessels and left her in the dungeon's bath to die.

The horrifying news spread quickly in the city. When Baktash became aware of this shocking and painful incident, he jumped on his horse and hurried to the palace. The guards tried to stop him, but Baktash defeated them one by one. He entered the palace and looked for Harith. Running for his life, Harith tried to escape but was killed. Baktash hurried to the dungeon but found Rabia gasping for life. She died in Baktash's arms. Filled with extreme anger and sadness, Baktash pulled his dagger and plunged it into his heart. This sad story of Rabia has been described by many great poets and mystics, including Sheik Farid al-Din Attar, Abu Saeed Abu al-Khair and Maulana Abdul Rahman Jami, as a Heavenly love.

Years passed and no one was aware of the existence of Rabia's grave and the underground bath where Rabia and Baktash were buried.

In 1960s, during the reign of King Mohammad Zahir Shah, Afghan historians and scholars discovered Rabia's burial place in the basement of an old building in the city of Balkh. The old building is located near the Shrine of Khwaja Abu Nasr Parsa, a 15th century Sufi and philosopher. The search was led by the renowned Afghan scholar Salahuddin Seljuki who found Rabia's poems written on the basement walls.

Tomb of Rabia and Baktash after Restoration

This was indeed a great discovery, proving the tragic life story of Rabia and her great love for Baktash.

Despite the fact that the event occurred 1,000 years ago, Rabia's memory has been seared in the hearts and minds of those who admired her moving and well-expressed poems. While bleeding to death in the underground bath, using her finger as a pen and her blood as ink, she wrote her last poetic verses on the wall of her dungeon:

Now agonized by the fire of passion
Dying from tears and bleeding
I am about to leave this unfair world
The world of cruelty and hatred
My life ended without seeing you
I wish you a long life
So, the story of our love
Will be told for centuries

Author's Note:

As a student at Sultan Razia High School in Mazar-e-Sharif, I was honored to be part of that historical and memorable event, the discovery of Rabia Balkhi's tomb. Thousands of students and key personalities from Mazar-e-Sharif high schools and neighboring provinces participated.

The opening ceremony was held in honor of Rabia Balkhi, the first female poet in our country. It was a great occasion. Many students who admired and loved Rabia Balkhi's talents and bravery were in tears as speakers gave speeches about her and the rare discovery of her tomb.

To me it was a blessed day to be there. The event took place in 1960 on an amazingly beautiful autumn day. The spirit of Rabia was with each and every one of us. This unforgettable gathering was attended by high-ranking government officials, professors, and Afghan historians, scholars from neighboring countries, journalists, and representatives of the Afghan Women's Foundation. Afghan and non-Afghan scholars presented in-depth and academic essays about Rabia's life, her style of writing, her inner thoughts and, of course, her notable personality.

Also, Rabia Balkhi's poems were recited by the students of Sultan Razia Girls School and her biography was presented by teachers and some of the students.

I was accompanied by my family in this grand ceremony. My older sister, Karima AbassFarani, chaired this assembly and my other sister, RohiaAbass Haidar, recited her poem on the topic of Spiritual Love.This day was one of the most enlightening experiences of my life, because all of us participants felt Rabia's presence and spirit.

Khojesta Herawi

Khojesta was from the highly cultured province of Herat. She was an educated young lady and a well-known poetess. She is also known as Khojesta of Sarakhs, the district where her father came from.

Khojesta spent most of her life in the city of Herat while regularly traveling to Balkh and Bukhara.

In the Thesaurus of Asadi, Khojesta is referred to as the most eloquent woman of her time, that is, during the Samanid era.

Khojasta's poems are famous for their frankness, sharp tongue, and serious tone despite the fact that she was continuously criticized for these attributes by her male contemporaries. In particular, Munjik and Ama'aq poets of Bukhara mocked her creative work and wrote sarcastic poems about her. It appears that some male poets of her era did not take female poets very seriously and ridiculed their literary work. However, their criticisms and sarcastic remarks did not deterKhojasta from continuing to produce unique poetry. Instead, she became more determined and decisive. Responding courageously to her critics, she clarified her position firmly and creatively through her poems with lucidity and no fear.

To the narrow-minded ones mocking me
Remember that I am a woman!
I can bake thousands of Munjik and Ama'aq
Like a little pie, made out of flour in my kitchen
Be aware if you step here carelessly
The boiling water may give you blisters
Be polite in my presence
Many vulgar people in this world
Indeed, come and go
But the ones with integrity
Are remembered with reverence

In historical texts, Khojasta is referred to as an articulate poetess. Compared to the soft, sophisticated and spiritual verses of Rabia Balkhi, her poems are very sharp, to the point, and sometimes filled with anger against discourteous men. Maybe the harsh assessment of her work by her male contemporaries made her to be this blunt and sharp. Or perhaps the tragic death of Rabia resulting from the male dominance of her time was the cause of her anger and disappointment.

References

Bois, Francois de (2004). Persian Literature - A Bio-Bibliographical Survey: Poetry of the Pre-Mongol Period (Volume V). Routledge.

Professor A. Habibi, 1985"A Consise History of Afghanistan"

Robinson, Chase F. (2009). The new Cambridge history of Islam. Vol 1, Sixth to eleventh centuries: Cambridge Univ. Press

Saffarid dynasty". The Oxford Dictionary of the Middle Ages. Oxford University Press". 2010.

Turchin, Peter; Adams, Jonathan M.; Hall, Thomas D (December 2006). "East-West Orientation of Historical Empires". Journal of World-Systems Research.

Mir Gholam M Ghobar "Afghanistan In The Course Of History Vol.2 in English

Renee Grousset, The Empire of the Steppes: A History of Central Asia, Transl. Naomi Walford, (Rutgers University Press, 1991),

Aftab, Tahera (2022). Sufi Women of South Asia: Veiled Friends of God

Blois, Francois de (2004). Persian Literature - A Bio-Bibliographical Survey: Poetry of the Pre-Mongol Period (Volume V).

Dabashi, Hamid (2012). The World of Persian Literary Humanism. Harvard University Press

Khwaja Parsa Complex Conservation". archnet.org.

CHAPTER FIVE

Famous Women of the Ghaznawids Era
11thand 12th century AD

At the end of the Samanid period, the beginning of 11th century AD, the Ghaznawids came to power and established a large empire that stretched from the Ganges River to the Persian Gulf and the Caspian Sea. The Ghaznawids monarchs controlled large parts of Persia, India, and Central Asia. During their reign, the Dari literature and poetry reached its zenith. Great poets, nurtured in the courts of the powerful Mahmud Ghaznawid and his descendants, contributed the most valuable works of poetry and prose to Dari literature and knowledge. Farrukhi, Unsuri, Asjudi and Firdausi were the greatest poets of this era.

Ghazni was home to the greatest scholars of the Islamic world. Abu Rayhan al-Biruni and Abu Ali Sina Balkhi (Avicenna) also known as Ibn e Sina, authored the most important scientific works of this era. Their books are still used by scientists and thinkers around the world. Firdausi's Shahnamah was born in the city of Ghazni.

Historical sources make reference to the many diverse activities of women of this period, including participation in political and administrative affairs; acquisition of knowledge; and pursuing the study of science, literature, mathematics, and even astronomy.

In the works of art and handicrafts of the Ghaznawid era, we can see the important role that women have played. Similarly, women contributed to the field of decorative arts and the development of the delicate metalworking industry, for which Ghazni was world famous at that time. As it is reflected in the artifacts of this era, the role of women was essential in this creative development. Most of the delicate works of art such as tapestry, ceramic dishes, and especially the exquisite metal utensils of Ghazni were created with the advice and taste of the ladies of Ghazni.

Ghazni was known as the bride of the cities during the reign of Sultan Mahmud and his descendants, Sultan Massoud, Sultan Ibrahim, Bahram Shah and Massoud III. This historic city with its magnificent palaces, towering minarets, crowded markets, numerous libraries, well-equipped baths, and beautiful gardens was considered one of the most civil societies in the Islamic world. In this big and populous city, skilled and

47

active women played a major role in the politics and administrative affairs of the country. Among them, HorraKhutali is one of those notable women.

Horra Khutali

Horra Begum Khutali was the daughter of Amir Sabuktagin and the sister of Mahmud Ghaznawi. She was one of the most powerful and famous women of this era. According to the distinguished historian of this period, Baihaqi, anyone who had encountered her attested to her wisdom, intelligence, and ingenuity. In her own special way, when making important political decisions, she would consult the great sultans of Ghazni. She even played an important role in the removal of key government officials.

Horra Begum Khutali's influential character, dignified personality, and prudent decisions played a major role in resolving conflicts between the country's different ethnic groups. Muhammad al-Utbi, the author of Yamini history, writes:

"King Sabuktagin had several daughters. But, Horra had special wisdom and skills that made her stand out among all the women [who] lived in the harem. She was an independent and influential young princess when all other women faced serious restrictions. It should be noted that the powerful sultans of Ghazni sought her opinion on most important issues such as war or reconciliation with the kings of other countries."

Her advice was generally helpful in keeping the vast Ghaznawid kingdom strong and powerful. Horra had a self-reliant and determined personality which allowed her to establish a successful working relationship with her brother, Sultan Mahmud. Horra also played a significant role in keeping peace and order in the powerful Ghaznavid Empire, while working closely with her brother, Sultan Mahmud.

Abu al-FadlBaihaqi, the 11th century renowned historian, speaks highly of Lady Horra Khutali's ability to maintain order under pressure. For example, despite her immense grief due to Sultan Mahmud's death, she did not lose her calm. She ordered that all ministers and courtiers not to reveal the great Sultan's death to the public until Prince Massoud returns from a trip abroad.

When Prince Massoud arrived in Ghazni, everything regarding Sultan Mahmoud's burial was ready; she had arranged the service very efficiently and had prepared the foundation of a glorious mausoleum.

Upon her written recommendation, Sultan Massoud built the tomb of Sultan Mahmud in the Garden of Firouzi, where the late Sultan used to meet with his court poets and scholars. Mahmud is held in high respect and his shrine continues to be visited by those who still remember him.

The Mausoleum of Sultan Mahmoud Ghaznawid

Lady Horra Khutali had great power and influence during the rule of Sultan Massoud. When Prince Masoud assumed power, he respected Lady Khutali as much as his father did. She was his noble aunt, who in fact led him to the throne and supported his kingdom. Like his father, Sultan Massoud sought her advice in important political and civil matters.

Horra Khutali was a prominent woman. Despite her fame and important role in the courts of the Ghaznawid kings, historians have written very little about her family life or her children. Only in the notes of al-Utbi, it is mentioned that Horra Khutali was married to a gentleman named Abu al-Hassam Ali ibn Mamun, who was a local ruler. None of the historians has mentioned the names of her children.

At that time, many political marriages were held to strengthen the foundations of kingdoms, and perhaps the marriage of Horra Khutali was one of those marriages. In support of this idea, the great historian of the Ghaznawid era, Baihaqi writes that political marriages were common among the families of the Ghaznawid kings, the Seljuk and the Khwarizmi dynasties.

Horra Khutali would accompany Sultan Massoud when he decided to invade India. Historians believe that her advice was very beneficial to the young Sultan because of her experience and her knowledge gained from association with her father Amir Sabuktagin and her brother Sultan Mahmud. Horra served as an adviser in her nephew's court until she reached an old age.

The historical documents of the Ghaznawid era show that HorraKhutali was the most outstanding, determined, and dedicated lady in the political history of Afghanistan. She died in the year 1083 AD.

Bastagin Begum

Bastagin Begum was also an influential lady in the court of Ghaznawid kings. A powerful and dignified lady in the court of Sultan Massoud, she was highly respected for her skills and talents. According to Baihaqi, she was trained by her mentor, Lady Horra Khutali, to assist her with her busy schedule. Her work with Lady Horra was the cause of her promotion to the court of Ghaznawid monarchs. Guided by the wisdom of her role model, Horra, Bastagin would often give advice in managerial affairs. It is said that Sultan Massoud viewed her as a kind lady, and valued her opinions and skills. After Horra Khutali, Bastagin Begum was the second most powerful and prominent woman in the court of Sultan Massoud.

As the historians of the Ghaznawid era report, Bastagin Begum would prepare the most delicious food for the court of Sultan Mahmud and arrange the royal banquets. She had gathered the best recipes and had recruited the most talented cooks from the vast regions of Ghaznawid Empire who would prepare the food under her supervision. Having worked as a young child in the court of Sultan Mahmoud, she was considered very a trustworthy and faithful confidant who was given the charge of supervising and preparing various dishes in the court of Sultan Mahmud.

During this era, outside of the royal court, there were also many famous ladies in the city of Ghazni who were active in artistic innovations, poetry and scientific activities. Among them, Rayhana Ghaznawi is considered to be one of the most honorable women of Afghanistan in science and literature.

Rayhana Ghaznawid

This very I intelligent and highly educated young lady lived in the reigns of Sultan Mahmud of Ghazni and Sultan Massoud. Abu Rayhan al-Biruni speaks of her with great admiration in his book Al-Tafhim, or Educating. Rayhana was a student of Al-Biruni and benefited a great deal from the knowledge of this most prominent and well-known scholar, philosopher, geographer, and mathematician of the Islamic world.

Perhaps Rayhana was one the most fortunate girls of her era due to Al-Biruni from whom she learned about astronomy, basic sciences, math, and physics. During their association, Rayhana would assist the great scholar in his scientific projects and academic research. As a consequence of this association, Rayhana became a learned young lady who would later assume the role of a teacher to other young students, both male and female.

Rayhana's father, Khwarizmi, was also considered a scientist and a scholar who would have interesting scientific discussions with Abu Rayhan al-Biruni. Being a very smart and highly motivated young girl, youngRayhana would always try to listen to these engaging conversationsfor deeper understanding of scientific and literary issues of the day. Daily there would always be something new to learn from these exchanges between Biruni and her father. Historical notes of the Ghaznawid era indicate that many students in the city of Ghazni learned complex mathematical equations and other scientific concepts of that time from Rayhana. In addition to mathematics and sciences, Rayhana was quite familiar with the field of literature and poetry. As a teacher, she would also work on grammar and writing skills with her students.

A Page from Scientific Studies of Al-Beruni and his Students

RayhanaGhazanwid was indeed one of the most important female scientists of Afghanistan in the 11th century AD. But regrettably not much research has been done on her life story by Afghan scholars, and many Afghans are not aware of her scientific accomplishments. As a progressive person, she was ahead of her time. Even in Europe, there weren't many women of her caliber during the medieval times.

Sisters of Sultan Ibrahim

During the reign of Sultan Ibrahim, great poets such as MassoudSa'adSalmaan and SanaieGhaznawi wrote the most eloquent poetry. Similar to the progressive city of Baghdad of that era, Ghazni was still the center of arts and literature, but for a brief period, a serious threat shook the powerful Ghaznawid Kingdom. Tughral, one of the slaves of Ghaznawid dynasty, rebelled against the Ghanawid dynasty. Tughral and his followers attacked the imperial palace in the middle of the night and imprisoned the royal family, including forty women of the royal family. Minhaj Siraj Jawzjani, the historian of this period, reports that Sultan Ibrahim and his brother Farrokhzad were also locked up along with their wives, sisters, and daughters.

Among the sisters of Sultan Ibrahim, Razia Begum, nicknamed Noorton Khatun, was a spiritual and faithful young lady. It is said that when one of Tughral's officers ordered the killing of every member of the royal family, Razia smiled with confidence and asked God for forgiveness. While everyone feared their probable death, miraculously an officer entered the dungeon and assured the prisoners that he was not going to kill anyone, since all of a sudden, he felt that it was far from justice to kill innocent people. Instead, he delayed the execution of the royal family until Tughral was arrested by the loyal generals of the Ghaznawid dynasty.

All the captives were rescued, and Sultan Ibrahim was very touched by Razia's confidence and her strong faith in the Divine power.

Minhaj Siraj reports that his grandfather had married one of the sisters of Sultan Ibrahim. God Almighty answered the prayers of one of the princesses, and upon God's mercy their nightmare ended.

Sultan Ibrahim became the powerful ruler of Ghaznawid Empire after his brother Farrokhzad. He was a thoughtful and peace-loving person who established good relations with the Seljuk kings. After the marriage of Gowhar Khatun, the beautiful Seljuk princess to Massoud III, Sultan Ibrahim's son, a period of peace began between the Ghaznawid and Seljuk dynasties.

During this time Sanaie was the most favored poet of his court. He was poised, well-dressed and very articulate. It is said that among all the writers, Sanaie, with his stature and delicate poetic nature, was highly regarded and admired by most of the women in the palace. It is said that one day, while passing by a poor neighborhood in luxurious clothes, Sanai encountered a drunkard dervish named Sayed Laykhar, singing nonsensical words and phrases. Sanaie glared at him and shook his head regretfully. The dervish looked at him and said sarcastically, "What you do in the king's court is worse than what I do in the streets. Why don't you praise God instead of praising the king and pleasing beautiful women?"

It is said that the words of the mourning dervish had such an effect on Sanaie that he threw away his luxurious clothes and would no longer attend the royal banquets.

After this incident, Sanaie went into seclusion and started meditation. He wrote his masterpiece while describing the Divine Power in the world of creation and the spirit of human devotion to the Creator.

At the royal court, everyone was worried about Sanaie and his absence. Sultan Ibrahim was also concerned. However, Razia's grief was very great. Thus, Sultan Ibrahim decided to go to see him personally to bring him back to his court. But Sanaie did not accept the invitation and instead recited these verses to him.

I am not a man who cares for gold and women
If you even give me your crown,
With all due respect,
I will not take your crown

Sultan Ibrahim returned to the palace in despair and told his sister that Sanaie would no longer come to the court. She was very disappointed to hear this news. A poem in response to Sanaie's rejection and attributed to Sultan Ibrahim's sister, elaborates on the situation as follows:

What excuse can you bring beforeGod?
When you took the path of love without me?
The night is dark and the road is rough,
It is a pity that you traveled without guidens

In response to her, Sanaie wrote:

Response
Your wavy hair had trapped me for a while
While your sleepy eyes made me sleepless
Now your sardonic lips are mocking me
But I am on a journey to find myself

This story is based on local narratives, not supported by historical documents, however. Some people have accused Sanaie for being prejudiced against women since he said, "I am not a man who cares for women," meaning that he was not the type of man to brag about having relationships with multiple women and showing off his wealth, prestige, and status. However, it is clear that Sanaie did not promote the idea of "Misogyny".

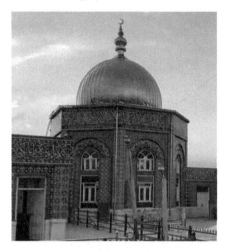

Sanaie's Tomb in Ghazni

Sanaie is recognized to be a Sufi poet. Like other spiritual poets andSufi thinkers, he had great respect for pioneer women such as Rabia Al-Adawia, Maryam Basri, and others who lived a life of service to God and humanity and who guided society in the right path.

Sultan Ibrahimand and all his sisters donated a large portion of their wealth and personal property to charities and needy people. When they went to Mecca for the Hajj pilgrimage, they contributed large sums of their own funds to the maintenance of Ka'aba and the poor communities of Mecca. For that reason, Sultan Ibrahim and his sisters became symbols of kindness and generosity of their time.

If we view the general culture of the Ghaznawid era through the mural paintings and the artwork, women played significant roles in society.

The sculptures and paintings discovered from Sultan Massoud palaces in Ghazni, Lashkar-gah in the Helmand Valley, and Takht-e Safar in Herat, all show women's status and important roles in society.

The metalwork and porcelain industry of Ghazni had reached its zenith, and the women's artistic taste and images are clearly portrayed in these beautiful historical artifacts. It is unfortunate that the names of the women artists are not mentioned in these artifacts.

Samples of Ghaznawid's Period Artifacts

References:

Professor A. Habibi, 1985"A Consise History of Afghanistan"

Mir Gholam M Ghobar "Afghanistan In The Course Of History Vol.2 in English

Bosworth, C. Edmund (31 August 2007). Historic Cities of the Islamic World. BRILL.

Mohammad Habib (1981). K. A. Nizami (ed.). Politics and Society During the Early Medieval Period: Collected Works of Professor Mohammad Habib. People's Publishing House.Chandra, Satish (2004). Medieval India: From Sultanat to the Mughals-Delhi Sultanat (1206-1526)→Part One. Har-Anand Publications→C.E. Bosworth, "The Ghaznavids: 994–1040", Edinburgh University Press, 1963

Rahman, H. U. (1995), A Chronology of Islamic History: 570 – 1000 CE, London: Mansell Publishing,

Lindberg, David C. (March 1980). Science in the Middle Ages. University of Chicago Press.

CHAPTER SIX

Elite Women of the Ghurid Period

The Soaring Minaret of Jam
Ghore, Afghanistan

The Ghurids were an ancient dynasty from Ghor Province in western Afghanistan. Their empire began in the mid-eleventh century AD in the capital city of Firozkoh. In less than a century, their power expanded from Firozkoh eastward to Bengal, and to Merv and Neyshabur in the north.

The Ghurids were famous for making excellent weapons and for being very strong militarily despite their highly cultured people and advanced civilization. During this era, many famous scholars and poets such as JebliGharjestani, Malek Shah Gharshin, (the Pashto poet), Minhaj Siraj Jawzjani (a famous historian of this era), and BahauddinWalad, father of MowlanaJalaludin Balkhi "Rumi" lived in the city of Balkh in today's Afghanistan.

While the positive role of influential queens and princesses of the courts of the Ghurid dynasty was significant, they played important roles in the cultural advancement of their era. Being encouraged by the powerful kings and queens of Ghor, the women's accomplishments were remarkable in advancing the sciences, arts, and literature. Besides its natural charm in the high mountainous land of Ghor, Firozkoh was the center of cultural achievements; magnificent palaces; and splendid towering minarets. Built in honor of Sultan GhiyasUd DinGhurid, the Minaret of Jam was one the tallest minarets in the Islamic Worldof its time.

The Minaret of Jam was decorated with Sūrah Maryam from Chapter 19th of the Holy Quran, embossed in Kufic script.

According to several archeologists, the choice of Qur'anicSūrah Maryam, Holy Mary, the mother of Prophet Jesus, indicates that the Ghurid kings and queens not only honored all prophets but highly respected women and held mothers in high esteem.

Despite their busy social lives inside their homes and outside in the courts, the Ghurid women enthusiastically participated in educational activities. Among them Queen Kaidan, served her people as a very powerful queen.

Queen Kaidan

This powerful and influential lady was one of the first queens of the Ghurid dynasty. Queen Kaidan was the daughter of King Bedridden Kaidani, the mother of Sultan Ghias-ud-Din Muhammad Sam and Sultan Mu'izz al-Din Muhammad Sam. She had three daughters who also went on to become famous queens of Khurasan and Central Asia. Queen Kaidan first lived in the Sangha area of Ghor province and then moved to Firozkoh. Known as the Queen of the Mountains and nicknamed as the Queen of the World, indicates that the Ghurid women had considerable power in the medieval times. Queen Kaidan provided her children with outstanding education, teaching them to be fair rulers and dedicated servants of society. She herself was fond of reading, spending most of her time in her study room, reading books on religion and history.

The family tree of the Ghurid sultans is complex due to the similarities and repetition of the names but every child born to this powerful queen ruled over a large region and left a mark on the history of this region and of the times.

According to Minhaj Siraj, the famous historian of this era,

Queen Kaidan had in her possession the most complete text of the Ghurid dynasty's genealogy, which she held onto with great care. Queen Kaidan was in constant contact with her two sons who were powerful rulers and her three daughters who were influential queens. Her most famous daughter was Queen Horra Jalali, not to be mistaken with Horra Khutali of Ghazni.

Queen Horra Jalali

Horra literally means a "free woman". In this era, the title "Horra" referred to "independent women" who were not restrained or enslaved by anyone. It also meant brave and free-spirited women. Queen Horra Jalali was one such woman. She was a lady of high caliber who ruled with wisdom and good judgment; she was very much interested in scientific discoveries and cultural activities.

Her son Sultan Baha'u'llah II was a great ruler, and like his mother, this powerful queen lived in the late eleventh and early twelfth centuries AD. She donated large sums of money for building bridges and irrigation dams to help farmers. She also built guest houses for caravans in Ghor, Nimroz, and Farah provinces so that travelers and merchants would have places of rest during their long journeys. Moreover, she also established a number of madras to educate children. Queen Horra was a literate woman, eager to learn, and provide educational opportunities for girls inside her palace.

After many centuries, Queen Horra Jalali is still remembered with great respect. Most recently in today's Charikar in Parwan Province, the Ministry of Education named a school in her honor as Horra Jalali High School.

The Students of Hora Jalali High School in Parwan Province

In the last few years, the students of Horra Jalali High School have had several scientific exhibitions and have demonstrated their discoveries in the fields of applied sciences, geography, and computers. They have also held seminars on Islamic studies, painting, and language arts.

The cultural activities of Queen Banu Horra Jalali became a source of inspiration for the rest of the influential women in the Ghurid Royal dynasty, among whom PrincessJowhar Malek Mah Banu stood out as a very inspired woman with many good deeds for her society.

Queen Jowhar Malek

Queen Jowhar Malek, nicknamed as Taj-e-Harir, (The Lady with the Silk Crown) was one of the mightiest queens of the Ghurid dynasty. She was the daughter of Sultan Ala-ud din and the wife of Sultan Ghias al-Din Sam, the most powerful king of Ghor.

Queen Taj-e-Harir was famous for her beauty and charm. Her popularity extended from Bust to Zaranj, from Ghor to Badghis, and from Herat to Balkh. People loved her because she believed in justice and in assisting the poor. In her palace, she had a large guest house where once a week she held court for the common people to be heard and be given a chance to speak to their beloved queen. The queen would listen to them from behind her silk curtains and would help them with their issues to the extent possible.

Portrait of Sultan Ghias-u-Din

It is said that Sultan Ghias-ud-Din built a huge garden in the Helmand province to entertain himself, his children, and his wife. The garden was built for the pastime and entertainment of the royal family. It was named the "The Garden of Serenity ".

The Garden was adorned with the most beautiful decorative trees, such as pine, spruce, willow, sycamore and fruit trees. Streams of water, fountains, and colorful flowers added to its beauty.

In the corner of the garden was a beautiful recreational palace where Queen Jowhar Malek, her sons, and daughters, and her grandchildren gathered and rested. Minhaj Siraj writes that no king had a garden that would match the beauty of the "Garden of Serenity".

Sultan Ghias-ud-Din, a keen hunter, connected the Garden of Serenityto a large hunting ground that was several miles wide. At the king's order, the hunting grounds were populated with thousands of deer, mountain rams, beasts, and colorful birds, so that the king and his courtiers could hunt and enjoy the beauty of the place while hunting. As one would assume, the compassionate queen with her kind heart was not very happy with her husband's decision. She didn't want to see the beautiful birds and deers killed just for the king's pleasure. Thus, she decided to do something about it to save the lives of the animals. He asked Fakhr-ul din Mubarak, the court poet, to write an insightful passionate poem that would stop the Sultan from killing the animals. But instead, Fakhr-ul din Mubarak who knew the Sultan's personality wrote a symbolic poem. He recited the poem to him while he was getting ready to go hunting. The poem reads as follows:

Oh, dear Sultan, why are you running after the mountain deers?
Don't you know that you have a Heavenly Lady here at home?
Alas her beautiful heart bleeds,
When your arrows bleed the heart of living creatures.

The Court Poet Reciting His Poem to Sultan by The Order of the Queen

By listening to the message of the poem, Sultan Ghias-ud din realized that his hunting was causing his beautiful wife unhappiness. Consequently, he abandoned the practice.

Discouraging the king from hunting has been seen as a benevolent act and the first important step towards preserving the environment and protecting wildlife.

Similarly, having been dedicated to the education of Princess Malek Mah Banu is viewed as a remarkable act in promoting education for females in the history of Afghanistan.

Princess Mah Banu

This remarkable young princess was the well-educated daughter of Sultan Ghias-ud din Sam. Professor A. Habibi, the famous Afghan historian, refers to her as a very dedicated and highly educated lady:

"Princess Malek Mah, also calledMah Banu was a very active young lady who had a great deal of interest in philosophy, theology, history, and astronomy. She was young, full of energy, and very close to her father, the powerful Ghurid Sultan. The Sultan himself was a very knowledgeable man and supported his daughter to pursue her dreams".

Growing up in the highly sophisticated, mountainous culture of Firozkoh, the Princess was raised in a learned society where she became an avid learner as a child. The city of Firozkoh with its splendid palaces, academic institutions, and a meeting place for great Islamic scholars and scientists was a perfect environment for her educational pursuits. During this era, philosophy, theology and astronomy in particular had progressed to an advanced level. The Ghouid princes and princesses themselves, including Malek Mah Banu, were very much interested in the science of astronomy. They would all gather in the observatories to watch the stars and learn about the wonders of the universe. The clear sky of Firozkoh provided a perfect opportunity for this exciting scientific exploration. Fascinated by the magnificence of the universe, they all praised the glory of God. Perhaps, for this reason, Jebali, the court poet of the Ghorid Density, who usually accompanied the princes and the princesses, wrote these verses to describe his feelings about the glory of the universe:

During endless nights when I gaze at the infinite skies
The charm of the stars brings tears to my eyes

During this time, Minhaj Siraj Jawzjani, who he was the supervisor of several academic foundations, writes:

"Princess Mah Banu was a pioneer for the advancement of education. In fact, she was a role model for all the youth who were interested in learning general sciences of that era. At the request of princess, her father, Sultan Ghias al-Din gave her the financial support to build a large madrasa that would serve hundreds of students for higher education."

The historical documents of this era confirm that around 1163 AD, an enormous madrasa (Academic Institution) was built in the neighboring province of Badghis under the direct supervision of Princess Mah Banu.

The madras was known as the Shah of Mashhad Madrasa, an impressive educational center of its time. This enormous school was built in the ancient province of Badghis. Here, students learned Islamic law, mathematics, astronomy, medicine, geometry, and literature.

According to Professor Habibi, during the recent excavations and archeological studies, a stone inscription was found at the foot of the wall of this large school, in which the name of Malek Banu, daughter of Sultan Ghiyasud Din Ghurid, was engraved as the founder of this educational institution. Although this inscription has been damaged due to passage of time, it is still legible and shows Princess Malek Mah Banu as the founder of this grand academic center.

The feminine construction style of the Shah Mashhad Madrasa, especially with its delicate floral decorations, shows that the school was built under the princess' guidance and supervision.

The Remnants of Shah-e-Mashhad Madras in Badghis

It is said that upon the completion of the building, Princess Mah Banu invited the most experienced teachers and scholars from Herat, Ghor, Ghazni, Balkh, and the rest of the country to provide students with the best education possible. Malek Mah Banu was greatly respected by her peers and was considered a pure, benevolent, devout and resourceful person.

Princess Mah Banu never married; instead, she devoted her life to the service of her people with great love and devotion to fulfill her social duties for the sake of Almighty God.

Tabaqat-e-Nasiri by Minhaj Siraj Josijani refers to her as the most modest and graceful princess with a personality beyond description. She would travel to many cities, including Herat, Bost and Bamiyan to oversee the progress of education in the madrasas being built during her father's reign. She monitored the quality of education in each school to make sure that the students received proper education. Despite being the daughter of a powerful emperor, she remained a humble servant of God and worked as a dedicated educator all her life.

Towards the end of the mid-11th century, the Ghurid monarchs started to expand their territories eastward toward the Indian subcontinent. During this time, many Afghan families including military generals and intellectuals began to immigrate to India. Princess Razia was one among them.

Queen Sultan Razia

Sultan Razia was the first powerful queen in Islamic era who ruled large territories of the Indian subcontinent. She was the daughter of Sultan Shams ud-Din Iltutmish. Shams u-Din was from Ghazni but served in India as one of the key officials of the Ghurid sultans. Later he ruled over the vast parts of northern India with great fame and power. In order to know the ways and reasons for his rising to power in India, a study of the historical events of that time is necessary.

Shams ud-Din Iltutmish was a young man who had received military training in Ghazni and had spent some time in Bukhara. He was a man who had seen the world and had sufficient knowledge and administrative skills to be a successful governor. When he was deployed to Delhi, he worked under the command of Qutbuddin Aibak, the general of the Ghurid sultans. General Aibak, who later became a king, found him to be a very honest and dedicated individual and liked his sincerity in performing his duties.

Qutbuddin Aibak was originally from Samangan and ruled India as the vassal king of the Ghurid Sultans. Earlier in his life, he was a slave in the courts of Ghurids. As a polite, brave soldier, and a very skilled horseman, he became a successful general who conquered India. He admired and appreciated people with modesty and honesty; he had observed these very same attributes in Shams ud-Din Iltutmish and named him his successor after his death.

Iltutmish brought his wife and children from Ghazni to Delhi, and that's when Razia moved to India. Razia was very dear to her father because of her polite manners and intelligence. She spent most of her time with her father, learning every aspect of life from this highly educated man. Iltutmish was an experienced politician and a sensible statesman. He taught his daughter how to run the government and be a problem solver. From her father, Razia learned about the day-to-day affairs of running the different branches of the government. Iltutmish was a just man who treated people equally regardless of their race, religious affiliations, or social status. As a result, he earned the title of the Righteous King by the people of India. As always, Razia was very proud of her father, especially when he built the tallest minaret of Delhi in honor of Qutbuddin Aibak, the man who made him a sultan. The Delhi Minaret and the Palace of Lall Qala (The Red Palace) is still reminiscent of that glorious era when Razia was a young and caring princess.

As a child, Razia enjoyed learning Islamic subjects, mathematics, literature, politics, and martial arts. During this time, Khwaja Mu'in al-Din Cheshti, who was originally from Herat, brought Islamic music to India. He was a highly honorable Sufi whom Sultan Iltutmish respected highly. Razia grew up in an environment which was a fine blend of Afghan and Indian culture. She was greatly interested in music and poetry, and every now and then she would write her own poetry.

As Sultan Iltutmish was getting older, Razia was becoming a charming princess that everyone admired for her influential personality. The young princess had all the qualities that a ruler should have. For this reason, whenever the sultan traveled, he would appoint Razia as his viceroy. When Sultan Iltutmish was assured of her leadership qualities, he ordered his minister, Taj al-Mulk, to officially announce Razia as the Crown Princess and the future Ruler of India, a statement which angered Razia's older brother, Rokun al-Din Firuz Shah. Immediately after King

Iltutmish's death in 1254 AD, Firuz Shah managed to become king with the help of the courtiers who did not consider a woman's kingdom worthy.

Although Razia was the official crown princess, she congratulated her brother and did not object to his maneuvering. But Firuz Shah, who was a selfish man with interest in material comforts, offended the courtiers with his unacceptable ways of ruling. His negligence and incompetence were the cause of his subjects' uprising; some of his generals besieged the city of Delhi, which terminated not only his, but the rule of the Iltutmish dynasty.

The influential people of Delhi's court didn't have any choice but to apologize to Razia for their poor decision regarding her brother and wanted her to be the ruler.

While Razia's incompetent brother was imprisoned by the court officials, Razia accepted their request on the condition that government officials obey all God's commands and work in the best interest of the people. The courtiers and officials accepted Razia's request, and the coronation ceremony of Queen Razia took place in 1265 AD in Delhi. Thus, Razia earned the title of Sultan and was the first Afghan woman to become the empress of the Indian subcontinent.

After establishing order, peace, and calm in the country, she focused on promoting education. Historical records indicate that Sultan Razia bravely and seriously carried out the important tasks of running the government. However, in a patriarchal society, it was not easy for a woman to lead a vast kingdom. Thus, some of the arrogant courtiers who did not believe in women as leaders opposed her behind the scenes.

Portrait of Sultan Razia, by Indian Artists

The opposition became even stronger when Razia minted coins in her own name instead of her father's. The influential courtiers became even more upset when she promoted her loyal Abyssinian black slave[4], Yaqout, to the rank of a military general. These bold actions caused more opposition against her. But Razia did not pay much attention to their trivial complaints. Instead, in all military campaigns, she wore military gear and marched in front of the army.

Conversely, one of the most important events that took place during her reign was the revolt of Malek Tunia, the governor of "Tabar" or Bhatinda (in southwest Punjab). Malek Tunia had considerable military power, but the young queen did not fear him. She marched against him while loyal general Yaqout was behind her in this difficult battle. In this battle Yaqout was killed, which was one of the reasons for Sultan Razia's army's defeat. Malek Tunia captured Razia and imprisoned her in the dreadful Tabarhinda Castle's detention center. After a while, observing Razia's poise, noble behavior, patience, endurance, and intelligence, Malek Tunia madly fell in love with Razia and proposed marriage to her. Razia asked for some time to think. After making sure that he is sincerely in love with her, she accepted his offer.

Sultan Razia and her husband rushed to Delhi with a well-equipped army to regain her lost throne. But when they entered the city of Delhi, the military generals who did not like Malek Tunia started to resist. Meanwhile, the opportunistic statesmen encouraged the people of Delhi to revolt against Sultan Razia and Malek Tunia. As a result of their subversive campaign, Queen Razia and Malek Tunia were forced to retreat.These power struggles and a Hindu uprising at this time weakened the mighty kingdom of Muslim rulers of India. Malek Tonya and Sultan Razia were captured by the rebels and killed in 1258 AD.

Despite the ups and downs in Sultan Razia's political life, she tried her best to emerge as a brave ruler in a male dominated society. She is still remembered as a courageous leader and an eloquent poetess. These verses show her inner feelings as a woman:

I have happy sonnets on my lips

Although I have crows in front of me,

What is my fault?

Why should people kill me out of grief for no reason?

---

[4]Habesha people, mostly referred to Ethiopians and Eritreans'

.

I pardon them by the virtue of my royal wisdom

With intention to fly and do my service

Let's take a step back in the path of the past.

Haven't you heard the story of Farhad?[5]

References

Ahmad Ali Kohzad, History of Afghanistan, Vol II Persian Eddition, Kabul

Avari, Burjor (2013). Islamic Civilization in South Asia: A History of Muslim Power and Presence in the Indian Subcontinent

Bosworth, C. Edmund (2001b). "Ghurids". EncyclopædiaIranica, online edition, Vol. X,

Fasc. 6. New York.

Chandra, Satish (2004). Medieval India: From Sultanat to the Mughals-Delhi Sultanat (1206-1526) – Part One. Har-Anand Publications.

Ira M. Lapidus, A History of Islamic Societies 2nd ed. Cambridge University Press 2002

Schwartzberg, Joseph E. (1978). A Historical atlas of South Asia. Chicago: University of Chicago Press.

Muzaffar Husain Syed, ed. (2011). Concise History of Islam. Vij Books.

Peter Jackson (2003). The Delhi Sultanate: A Political and Military History. Cambridge University Press

Sudha Sharma (2016). The Status of Muslim Women in Medieval India.

Thomas, David C. (2018). The Ebb and Flow of the Ghūrid Empire. Sydney University Press.

Guida M. Jackson, ed. (1999). Women Rulers Throughout the Ages: An Illustrated Guide

---

[5] In Dari literature, Farhad is a legendary character who is the symbol ofsacrifice for a platonic love.

CHAPTER SEVEN

Afghan Women in the Thirteenth Century

In the 13th century AD, after Genghis Khan's attack on Islamic countries, great changes occurred in the Islamic world. At that time, as a result of the destruction, the economic and social situation was very disappointing, but with that description, there were important women in this period that should be mentioned.

Mo'mena Khatun[6], the Poised Lady of Balkh

Mo'mena Khatun is the mother of MowlanaJalaludin Mohammad Balkhi, known as Rumi in the West. She lived in a very critical era which corresponded with the raids of Genghis Khan whose conquests and raids were devastating to the Islamic countries. Genghis Khan's attacks and conquests caused great destruction and political changes in the Islamic countries, stretching from Bukhara to Baghdad.

Mo'mena Khatun was a calm and collected lady who did her best to keep her family safe and protected during these hostilities. Rumi was a teenager during this difficult time. His father BahauddinWalad was an important man in the city of Balkh. He was titled as Sultan al-Ulama, (The Master or King of all Scholars.) However, he had strong disagreements with Mohammad Shah, king of Khwarizm, who was a cruel, arrogant and an unjust ruler. Despite Mo'mena Khatun's good attempts to convince her husband not to provoke the tyrant king, as a fair judge, BahauddinWalad couldn't ignore all the cruelties of the royal family.

His opposition to King Mohammad Shah and Queen Turkan resulted in his exile from Balkh. Thus, Mo'mena Khatun had to be extra careful to maintain calmness and comfort in her family and raise her children to the best of her ability during her husband's exile.

Bahauddin returned to Balkh after one year of being in exile. Upon his return, the elite of Balkh welcomed himand praised his wife'stolarence and paitents, while he was in exile.

---

[6]Khatun is a title for a recpected lady.

In 1222 AD, due to Khwarizm Shah's incompetence and cruelty, Genghis Khan, after capturing major cities of Central Asia and killing many people along the way, crossed the Oxus River and marched towards the city of Balkh.Thus, BahauddinWalad and his family had to leave their homeland and take refuge in Rum of Seljuk, in today's Turkey. They settled in the city of Konya. Despite her illness during their long trip from Balkh to Neyshabur and from there to Baghdad, and finally to Konya, Mo'mena Khatun was the most calm and collected member of the family. With her kindness, patience and wisdom, she was a great help and a reliable source of support for her husband and children during this long, difficult journey.

The ruins of MowlanaJalaludin's home in Balkh

It is said that on many occasions, the bandits would not harm their caravan because of her poise, kindness, and motherly demeanor. As a matter of fact, out of respect for Mo'mena Khatun, some of them would go out of their way to guard their small caravan. At night, when the caravan would stop for rest, she would recite poetry and tell the stories of prophets to her children. The poems of Mowlana clearly illustrate the notion of selfless love for the Divine and humanity, which is attributed to his mother's selfless behavior and Maulana's deep philosophical thoughts, on the same token comes from his father.

It is said that on the way to Konya, Momena Khatun encountered a beautiful and very gentle young lady, named Gowhar Khatun. Her family was from Balkh. Momena Khatun liked her and told her about her son Jalaludin, who was in his mid 20s at this time. Upon his mother's recommendation, MowlanaJalaludin Rumi married Gowhar Khatun. She gave birth to two healthy sons by the names of Baha Wald and Alauddin. However, she died at a young age, and Mowlana did not remarry for ten years out of respect for Gowhar Khatun.

When Rumi's family settled in Turkey, MomenaKhatoun would serve needy people and attend to her beloved grandsons. She would advise her genius son, Mowlana Rumi, on loving and respecting all mankind in order to please Almighty God. This was her belief until she passed away at an old age, but her noble thoughts and honest sentiments were always valued and remembered by her son and his followers.

Turkan Khatun

During this period, another woman named Turkan Khatun, the wife of Sultan Takosh and the mother of Mohammad Khwarezm Shah, had become a powerful queen. She lived in Khwarezm and ruled from the city of Organj in present-day Turkmenistan over a large area of Central Asia, Khurasan, and Persia. Historians have described her as a ruthless, cruel, and selfish woman.

The city of Balkh was under the control of Khwarizm Shah at this time and by the order of Queen Turkan, hundreds of scholars and freedom fighters were imprisoned and punished. This was the reason for BahaudinWalad's opposition to the rulers of this period. Several historical documents show that Turkan Khatun carried a royal seal with her, referring to herself as the Crown of the World and Religion. No power could challenge her decisions; whenever she gave a verdict to condemn someone, it was carried out without any opposition. Her son Mohammad Khwarazm Shah was just as cruel and selfish as his mother.

Turkan Khatun had an assistant named Tarkhan, who also happened to be her nephew. He did not refrain from any kind of oppression, aggression, and/or discrimination against common people, especially the Mongols.

American historian Nancy Dupree explains that when the Genghis's ambassador came to the court of Khwarizm, along with the merchants of Mongolia carrying many gifts, the arrogant Sultan of Khwarizm rejected their gesture for good relations. Several historians have stated that the Sultan ordered the murder of Genghis Khan's envoys. However, Queen Turkan went one step further; she confiscated all their property and ordered that they be killed in boiling water. The only person who escaped from her punishment was a 12-year-old Mughal boy who reported this horrifying news to Genghis. The infuriated Genghis retaliated by attacking the Islamic countries, and ruthlessly massacred thousands of innocent people.

Sultan Khwarizm fled to an island in the Caspian Sea where he was captured by Genghis Khan's soldiers and killed. However, Genghis did not kill Turkan Khatun; instead, he put a chain around her neck and made her walk behind his army.

The arrogant queen asked to be killed over and over, but Genghis refused to accommodate her wish. The arrogant queen would stand in a corner, watching Genghis Khan eating his meals. He would throw scraps of food and bones at her as he was eating. The mighty queen, who was feared by many people in her vast empire, ended suffering in humiliation during the final years of her life.

Henna Khatun

Henna Khatun was the daughter of Prince Jalaludin Khwarezm Shah and the spoiled granddaughter of Turkan Khatun. Like her grandmother, she was arrogant and selfish. During Genghis Khan's attack, she accompanied her father and took refuge in Balkh. Crossing the Amu River in pursuit of Henna, Genghis Khan's army entered the affluent city of Balkh in 1222 AD. It is said that Henna had brought with her the precious treasure of Genghis Khan, which was confiscated by her grandmother.

Genghis asked the people of Balkh to hand over Jalaludin and his daughter and that he would not attack their city. A tradition still valued in Afghanistan, that is, never to hand over a refugee to the enemy, the people of Balkh rejected his demand. The people of Balkh sent back the envoy of Genghis with no compliance to his demand. Furious with the peoples' response, Genghis ordered his troops to set Balkh on fire. The city was leveled to the ground and thousands were killed.

Prince Jalaludin and his daughter Henna Khatun escaped to Bamiyan and sought refuge with Malek Omar, the ruler of Bamiyan. Omar sheltered the Prince and his daughter with great honor and placed them in a nice palace on the hilltop with elevated towers, referred to as the Girl's Castle, the remains of which can still be seen

71

in Bamiyan. Genghis continued to chase father and daughter by besieging Bamiyan. But the fortification of the city was so strong that it took Genghis six months to conquer Bamiyan. During this time, Prince Jalaludin married the young daughter of the governor of Ghazni.

As a result of his father's unexpected marriage, Henna became very upset, and in a vindictive manner, decided to plot against them. In the dark of the night, she climbed one of the towers and with a bow and arrow in hand; she fastened a letter to the arrow and shot it to Genghis' army camp, revealing the underground passage to the city.

Genghis cheered with excitement. He entered the city easily that night. King Omar and his soldiers bravely fought back, but they were all killed. Prince Jalaludin escaped from Bamiyan, but Henna deliberately did not go with him. She waited until morning for Genghis. Princess Henna wanted to personally see him and ask for a big reward. But Genghis was in a grave mood that morning. He was extremely upset because his favorite grandson, Motochine, had been killed during the rage. He angrily ordered the killing of all Bamiyan residents. At this point, Henna Khatun came out of the palace gate and told Genghis that she is the reason for his victory, and that's why Genghis should make her his queen. Genghis madly laughed and replied: "You who betrayed the people who sheltered you and gave you amnesty, do not deserve any reward but death. I will kill you with no hesitation, so your story becomes an example for others."

Genghis killing Henna Khatun, and Burning the City of Bamiyan
By Ustad Ghusudin, Prominent Afghan Artist

72

Although Genghis brought death and destruction to the Islamic world, an age of reawakening started among the intellectuals. Many thinkers began to reevaluate the moral values of the society. After of Genghis Khan's attacks, since men were mostly killed in war and women were more involved in construction and agriculture, the idea arose that why women should be looked at as a weak gender. This reevaluation included the notion of men and women being of equal status with equal responsibilities; this concept was supported by religious scholars who proclaimed when men and women worship God, the Almighty God does not differentiate between men or women; thus, their status is the same as that of men whether they achieve goodness or fall in the swamp of sinfulness.

Rumi believed that the human soul is not a physical phenomenon to be defined in terms of gender (male or female) but beyond gender and beyond the values of the material world. Thus, no distinction should be made between men and women; men and women are interdependent beings, requiring reliance on each as the Providence calls for. He says:

Free your soul from your physical appearance
Since the soul of men and women come from one source

In spite of all the devastation caused by brutal wars, there were many brave women and men who rebuilt villages, farms, and cities.

The Al-Kurt dynasty, who was the descendants of the Ghurid kings, came to power and established their capital in Herat. These benevolent kings began rebuilding Herat and later, with the help of local people, started reconstruction of other locations including Zaranj, Farah, Helmand, Kandahar, Ghazni and Balkh.

References

Abul Hai Habib, "A Consise History of Afghanistan" Kabul Press

A Historical Atlas of Afghanistan, by Amy Romano,

Dictionary of Wars, by George C. Kohn,

The Conquests of Genghis Khan, by Alison Behnke,

Dictionary of Wars, by George C. Kohn

Tanner, Stephen (2002). Afghanistan: A Military History from Alexander the Great to the Fall of The Taliban. DA CAPO Press.

CHAPTER EIGHT

Afghan Women in the Timurid Era

In the middle of the fourteenth century AD, a mighty conqueror, Timur Korgani emerged from Central Asia. After his death, his son ShahrokhMirza chose Herat as his imperial capital. At the beginning of the 15th century, Herat became the center of science, art, poetry and literature as a result of the support and patronage of the Timurid dynasty. With the moral and financial support ofShahorkh Mirza and especially Queen Gowharshad, great artists, poets, architects, calligraphers and writers emerged in the vast territory of their kingdom. This period corresponded with the era of European Renceance.

Queen Gowharshad Begum

Queen Gowharshad Begum was a productive and selfless soul who elevated not only arts and literature but more importantly the status of Eastern women. She was considered the spiritual leader of all intellectuals and creative people of her time.

Gowharshad Begum was born circa 1410 AD., from the marriage of Lady Khan Zada and Ghiasuddin Agha.

Her father was a famous literary figure and a philosopher. He was considered one of the nobles of Herat with many admirers extending from Herat to Turkey.

Arab sources state that in 1416 AD, Gowharshad married Shahrokh Mirza, 12 years her senior, at the age of 16. From this marriage, Gowharshad gave birth to two daughters and five sons, three of whom are the very famous Ulugh Beg, Ruler of Samarkand, Baisonghor, Prince of Herat, and Ibrahim Mirza, Governor of Isfahan.

Unlike Timur, his warrior father, King Shahrokh was a peace-loving person. His taste in poetry, art, and literature was heavily influenced by Gowharshad Begum. As a result of his erudite wife's association, he supported a noble undertaking, that is, the start of the cultural renaissance of Herat during his reign. Soon, due to the great efforts of Queen Gowharshad, this cultural movement spread from the ancient city of Herat throughout the vast Timurid Empire.

Gowharshad's son, Prince Baysanghar, was a brilliant poet and calligrapher. The young prince, with the encouragement of his mother, established the first Academy of Fine Arts in the city of Herat, circa 1440s AD. More than forty of the best calligraphers and painters would be busy in the production of exquisite, illustrated poetry albums under the guidance of Queen Gowhershad and her son. Master artists, including book binders, miniaturists, and calligraphers created the classical poetry albums for the Royal Library of Herat. Queen Gowharshad would personally choose the book covers, adorned with gold leaf and embossed calligraphy. The book covers were usually made out of leather and gilded with delicate designs. She herself would examine each page carefully before they were chosen for the collection of The Royal Library of Herat. Queen Goharshad had great interest in illustration of the poetic stories such as "Laily and Majnoun, "Yusuf and Zuleykha," and other classical romantic and epic poems.

Her son, PrinceBaisonghor, on the other hand would usually review historical texts such as Iskandar Nama (Alexander's Life Stories) and Shah Nama (The Epics of Kings), which were all decorated with beautiful illustrations. The book covers were sometimes ornamented with precious stones such as rubies, turquoise, emeralds and azure under direct supervision of Queen Gowharshad. At every step of the production, her kind husband, Shahrokh Mirza, would support his wife's valuable efforts.

Queen Gowharshad also had great interest in architecture. Historian of Herat, Mir Khond, writes that the fortress of Qala Ikhtiareddin, once a military fortress and partially damaged by wars, was turned into a beautiful palace at the queen's recommendation. The western part of Ikhtiaruddin Castle, Arg of Herat, The Royal Palace of Herat, was rebuilt as Queen Gowhershad's residence palace.

This splendid building still stands tall with stylish elevated windows and connected hallways. Annually many visitors still enjoy seeing it.

A View of Queen's Residence in the Citadel of Herat

One of Gowharshad's greatest desires was to expand the city of Herat beyond the limits of the old city, known as Kuhan-dajh (The Old Castle). She proposed the idea to her wise and caring husband, Emperor Shahrokh Mirza, as a result of whose approval the foundation of the Mosalla Garden was laid.

With much enthusiasm, Queen Gowharshad began the construction of a magnificent garden, historically known as the Garden of Musalla. She invited the most experienced architects from Herat, including Ustad (Master) Zainuddin and Ustad Mohammad Banna, from Herat, and Quwam Shirazi, an experienced mason. Ibrahim Mirza Queen Gawharshad'sson, who was the governor of Persia, sent QuwamSherazi, to Herat to work directly under the queen's guidance.

The Queen's refined taste is evident in the design of the minarets, especially in the choice of colors and the delicate tile work of building structures.

The Garden of Mosalla&the Renaissance of Herat

This garden had a special splendor with its tall minarets decorated with its turquoise blue delicate tiles, rows of evergreen trees (Abies procera) and the Mausoleum of Queen Gowharshad with blue domed construction. The British traveler and writer Robert Byron, who visited Herat at the beginning of the nineteenth century, in his description of the Mosalla Garden writes:

"This is a garden of paradise that was created to the taste of a woman and was built by the most skilled architects for the worship of God. But how unfortunate, that it was destroyed by the British artillery with the hands of sinful men."

The erudite queen also ordered that a school of fine arts be built in her favorite garden, since she was very much interested in promoting the arts. Specifically, she wanted to build the school in memory of her artist son, Prince Baisonghor who had died at a young age due to excessive drinking. His tomb is located underground.

In 1447 AD, Shahrokh wanted to put down an insurgency in Persia, present-day Iran, and Gowharshad accompanied him since she didn't want to leave him alone on this unpleasant trip. Although Shahrokh managed to resolve the problem diplomatically, he fell ill and died in the vicinity of Tehran.

Even though there was a chance of uprisings, Queen Gowharshad managed the situation with utmost calmness, wisdom, and superb leadership that she had learned at a young age. On her way to Herat, Queen Gowharshad hired a well-equipped caravan and rode her horse next to her husband's coffin. While many soldiers were guarding the caravan, the bandits attacked the caravan and looted the king's valuables. Most of the soldiers were killed during the attack, but Gowharshad and her two grandsons bravely fought back. After many scuffles with the bandits, she managed to bring Shahrokh's body to the city of Herat. When they entered the city gate, no one was left alive from the caravan except for Queen Gowharshad, two bodyguards and her two brave grandsons, Allah al-Dawla and Ibrahim.

She held the memorial ceremony of her beloved husband in the city of Herat in the presence of thousands of people of Herat. King Shahrokh was buried next to his son, Prince Bisonghor, in the underground of the building, now named after Queen Gowhershad.

Queen Goharshad Begum and her husband ruled with utmost fairness and justice. After the death of her husband, this respected queen single-handedly carried out the important and difficult responsibilities of governing this vast empire with wisdom, compassion, and diplomacy.

Queen Gowharshad Begum ruled this empire from 1447 to 1457. The Timurid Empire during her rule stretched from Central Asia to Baghdad. Due to her fairness and compassion, she was considered as the spiritual leader and Mother of the city of Herat.

Queen Gowharshad's son, Mirza Ibrahim and her grandson, Allah al-Dawla were her assistants in many aspects of the empire's administrative and military affairs. They carried out government duties under the direct leadership of the Queen. In fact, Gowharshad was one of the few women in the Eastern world who emerged as a strong and well- respected leader. She paid special attention to poets and artists. During her rule, great artists such as Musa Musawer, Mirk Herawi, and MowlanaWali emerged as experienced trainers for the young artists and calligraphers of the time. Herat's prominent poet Abdurrahman Jami and most celebrated painter Kamaludin Behzad at a very young age were nurtured in their craft with the blessing of the Queen.

A View of Musalla Garden and Queen Gowhershad's Tomb

The Queen's selfless services included the expansion of trade, economical growth, and the advancement of culture, all of which were greatly admired and appreciated by the public. However, on June 19, 1457 AD she faced a serious and unexpected challenge which badly shook her government. Gowharshad was surprised by the military attack on the city of Herat by Sultan Abu Sa'id, a Timurid prince. The Queen tried to negotiate with him, but Abu Sa'id was firm on his decision and moved forward with his plan. Despite the Queen's courage and fierce resistance to defend the city, her forces were defeated, resulting in the death of her beloved grandson, Prince Allah al-Dawla, before her eyes. To stop further bloodshed,

Gowharshad surrendered and was cowardly executed despite Abu Sa'id's promise to let her live. Feeling guilty about the execution of a highly respected lady, Abu Sa'id agreed that Queen Gowharshad be buried in the basement of Musala Garden's building next to her son, Prince Baisonghor. Since that date this charming building has been called the mausoleum of Queen Gowharshad, the spiritual mother of the nation and the great supporter of arts and literature.

Mehri Herawi

In Gowharshad Begum's court, a woman poet by the name of Mehri Herawi would always accompany the Queen. They recited poetry together every night. Mehri Herawi had a happy life in the service of the Queen until her father married her off to a wealthy judge, named Abdul Aziz, who was much older than she. Mehri was extremely unhappy in this marriage because she had given her heart to the queen's young nephew, Massoud Tarkhan. Most of her poems were written about him. Masoud was aware of Mehri's love for him but, out of respect for his aunt, he would not say anything. Despite QueenGowharshad's awareness of Mehri's inclination towards Masoud, she did not realize the depth and magnitude of Mehri's love for her nephew until Massoud came to the court and Mehri recited the romantic poems that she had written for him. Massoud was very touched and so was the Queen, but it was too late to change destiny.

It was a sad moment for both Massoud and Mehri, but to change the tense atmosphere, Queen Gowharshad laughed politely and said to Mehri, "Love is something that does not know age and does not recognize status. I knew a blind dervish, who had never seen my face, but he was in love with me."

"He used to bring his Du-Taar (a string musical instrument) to the palace garden to serenade me. The guards wanted to stop him, but I would always say that he was a harmless man, and please let him sing since being in love is not a crime. As a matter of fact, it is a blessing. Sometimes, he would sing until late at night. One night my maids went to the garden and sat next to him while he was singing. The blind man stopped singing, and said, 'I bet, you are all as beautiful as the angels of paradise, but the person I love is not among you; in reality, she doesn't have to be next to me since she is always in my heart. And love is nothing, but a noble feeling.' GowharshadBegum paused for a moment and continued, "Sometimes we need to embrace our destiny, but it is important not to lose touch with our feelings."

Mehri continued to recite the other set of her poems, condemning arranged marriages. One the most eloquent poets of her era, Mehri composed very allegorical poetry, with intricacy that made it difficult to translate from Dari to English or any other languages.

Mehri's poems can be divided in two categories, her romantic poems and the verses she wrote to criticize some of the wrong societal traditions which made life miserable for women. Her poetry in classical style conveyed deep thoughts. Most of her poems have not been collected in the form of a published book, but the ones available are those printed in different magazines and periodicals.

Princess Shahrbanu:

Shahrabanu, the daughter of Sultan Abu S'aid, was one of the benefactors of her era. In the description of Shahrbanu, it is said that she was an enlightened lady, a lover of science and a promoter of arts. She was extremely generous and had a kind heart.

The AuqSaray Palace, which was built of white marble outside the city of Herat, was constructedunders her direct supervision. The palace had a special beauty and charming gardens. During this time, the irrigation canal that passed through the city of Herat made the gardens fresh. Shahrabanu personally supervised the irrigation work of the city; she was especially involved in the construction process of Takht-e Safar Garden and its pavilion. The building was decorated with the beautiful paintings of MowlanWali. These paintings portrayed Princess Shahrbanu's artistic taste and the cultural advancement of Heart under her patronage.

However, the city of Herat was full of bitter and sweet memories for her. Still many people, including Queen Gowhershad's grandchildren, and her admirers who disagreed with the cruel murder of the late queen by Abu Sa'id, were very upset. Thus, they started to revolt against him and gathered an army in the city of Sarkhas, in the north of Herat. Sultan Abu Sa'id also prepared for war with a large army to suppress his enemies.

Mirkhund, the renowned 15th century historian of Herat, the author of thebook *"Habib al-Sir"*, writes that when Sultan Abu Sa'id was preparing for war against his opponents, he advised his daughter Shahrbanu to go to Kabul to avoid the danger of war.

Thus, Shahrabanu came to Kabul. However, Sultan Abu Said was captured by the enemies in the battle of Qara-Bagh and was killed by Yadgar Muhammad, one of the great-grandsons of Queen Gowharshad, to avenge the blood of his grandmother.

Shahrabanu was deeply saddened to hear this news, but in order to keep her father's name alive in history, she built the immense garden of "Shahrara" which still exists in Kabul and is known as the Women's Garden. Of course, many changes took place in this garden in the following periods, but the main founder of this charming garden, which is dignated for women children, is Princes Shahrbanuthe daughter of Sultan Abu Saeed.

A view of ShahraraGarden in the City of Kabul

The women of the Timurid era were very interested in construction, following Queen Gowharshad Begum's steps. Queen Goharshad builtmany buildings in Balkh, like the Mausoleum of Khwaja Akasha and the magnificent gate of the central garden of the city Balkh. In the garden ofKhwaja Akasha, there is a big tree thatstands in the garden for 500 years. Acording to the people of Balkh, this tree was planted by Queen Gowharshad Begum.

There is also a jar in the museum of the *Fourth Caliph Mausoleum*inin the city of Mazar-e-Sharif, on which the image of Queen Gowharshad is painted, showing her popularity among the people of Balkh.

Firoza Banu

After the death of Sultan Abu Said, Sultan Hossein Bayqra, who was a man of culture and patron of arts, became the king. According to the opinion of the people of Herat, Sultan's mother, known as Firoza Bano, was keen on the construction of Khwaja Abu Nasr Parsa's Mosque.

The Mosque of Khwaja Abu Nasr Parsa

Abu Nasr Parsa was a spiritual leader as well as a great scholar. Hundreds of people in Balkh, Herat and other major cities of Afghanistan and Bukhara would gather to listen to him and learn from his profound and meaningful speeches. His discussions were philosophical, some of which would explore and ponder the true meaning of life. After Parsa's death in Balkh, Firoza Banu invited the most experienced masons to lay the foundation of his tomb and build a grand mosque in his honor in Balkh circa 1459 AD. She spent her own personal resources for the construction of the mausoleum. To symbolize his pure and free spirit, she wanted that, unlike most other tombs that were usually dark and somber, this mosque be well-lit with a radiant interior. Following her instructions, the masons designed the mosque with 16 windows and adorned its dome with blue turquoise tiles, to be reminiscent of Firoza Banu (Firoza in Dari means turquoise).This beautiful building is situated in the Central Park of Balkh. The tomb of Rabia Balkhi is also located in this park. This charming park is reminiscent of three famous ladies of Afghanistan: Rabia Balkhi, the first poetess in Dari literature; Queen Gowharshad; and Mother Queen Firoza Banu.

Khound Amir, the author of the major historical manuscript, "Habib al-siyar," writes that the women of the Timurid dynasty were keen supporters of artists, poets, and scholars and mentions Sultan Hessian's mother, Firoza Banu, who is still fondly remembered by the people of Balkh and Herat.

Beka Khatun

Beka Khatun was the erudite wife of Sultan Hussein Bayeqara and the mother of Prince Badi-ul-Zaman. Committed to education and increasing knowledge, she built several libraries in the city of Herat. Following the footsteps of Queen Gowharshad, she wanted to add more illustrated albums to the valuable book collection of Herat. Very interested in designing poetry books, she wanted manuscripts to be adorned with delicate illustrations. For this task, she invited Kamaluddin Behzad and his team, the best calligraphers and skilled bookbinders of the time, to create additional volumes under her supervision. Her special interest was in designing gilded and embossed margins. It is said that the most qualified students of Behzad were involved in creating fine margins for each page. She kept these valuable books in expensive boxes decorated with precious stones, such as ruby, lapis, and turquoise.

After the death of Sultan Hussain Bayeqra, Mohammad Khan Shaibani from present day Uzbekistan attacked the affluent city of Herat around 1510 AD. It is said that Prince Badi-ul-Zaman, during his escape, took a few volumes of these valuable books with him. Apparently, he gave a few volumes to Ismail Safavid, king of Persia in return for his hospitality and another set to the Ottoman Sultan as he eventually took refuge in Turkey. The Ottoman sultan was so pleased to receive such a valuable gift that he gave the prince amnesty and threw a royal party in his honor.

It seems that Beka Khatun moved to Kabul after the fall of Herat, and her son remained in Istanbul for the rest of his life. But Beka Khatun was still active while living in Kabul, laying the foundation of the gardens of Benafsha Bagh (The Violet Garden) and Mahtab Bagh (The Moon Garden).

Beka Khatun's name is mentioned in "TuzukJahangiri," (Memoirs of Emperor Jahangir), the famous ruler of India. The exquisite illustrated books that were created under her direct supervision are on display in the Topkapi Museum of Istanbul.

References

Abdul Hai Habibi 1976, "The art of the Timurid era and its miscellanyPublidhed in Tehran

Afghanistan Information Network >> General information. (Sultan Hossein Bayqra)

Barthold, VasiliiVladimirovitch (1963). Four Studies on the History of Central Asia. Vol. 2. Brill Archive

Jamaluddin, Syed (1995). The state under Timur: a study in empire building

Nancy H. Dupree, "Herat A Pictorial Guid, Afghan" Turist Organization, 1966

Ames, Christine Caldwell (2015). Medieval Heresies. Cambridge University Press.

Sultan Hossein Baiqara - The Great Islamic Encyclopedia

The Encyclopaedia of Islam, Brill Publishers, Vol.3: H-Iram, 1986, Leiden

Podelco, Grant (July 2005). "Afghanistan: Race to Preserve Historic Minarets of Herat,

Singh, Ganda (1959). Ahmad Shah Durrani, father of modern Afghanistan 2016-Asia Publishing

Noelle-Karimi, Christine (2014). The Pearl in Its Midst: Herat and the Mapping of Khurasan (15th-19th Centuries). Austrian Academy of Sciences Press.

CHAPTER NINE

Afghan Women in the Seventeenth Century

In the beginning of the 16th century AD, when Herat, the capital of the Timurid dynasty, was in a state of decline, Prince Zahir al-Din Babur, a descendent of Timur Korgani, established the base of his power in the city of Kabul in 1504 AD. Accordingly, Kabul became the center of political and cultural developments after the fall of the Timurids of Herat. In his diary, *Tuzuk e Baburi*, (The Memoirs of King Babur), he expresses his fascination with the refreshing climate and natural beauty of Kabul; he called it "paradise on earth". During this time, numerous artists, scholars, musicians, poets and influential people of Herat, including the wealthy Timurid princesses and highly cultured ladies, gathered in Kabul.

In the year 1657 AD, Babur conquered India by defeating Sultan Ibrahim Lodi who was killed in the battle of Panipat. After this big victory, Babur settled in the historical city of Agra, near Delhi. However, he would still visit Kabul since he wanted to maintain his ties with the people of Kabul. During this time many poets, artists, and musicians would accompany Zahiruddin Babur while stationed in India. Meanwhile, the increase in business resulted in more extended cultural ties between India and Afghanistan.

However, during this timeframe the supporters of Sultan Ibrahim Lodi, gathered around his wife, Shah Khanum Sultan Lodi, who was a brave and courageous woman. This was a serious threat to Babur's authority, since Ibrahim Lodi was originally from Afghanistan and still had many supporters in Ghazni and Kandahar.

Shah Khanum Sultan Lodi

Ibrahim Lodi's widow, nicknamed as Shah Khanum Sultan, was a distinguished and influential woman. She was very upset about her husband's death and endeavored to avenge Babur. Many influential personalities from India and Afghanistan, including military officers, still loyal to Ibrahim Lodi, were gradually gathering around her to overthrow King Babur. When Babur realized that this woman could cause him great trouble, he ordered her arrest and deportation from India to Afghanistan, and imprisoned her in Muzaffar Fort, Badakhshan, in the farthest corner of Afghanistan. It is said that she was captured in the middle of the night. Babar's soldiers put her on the back of a camel and headed for Afghanistan.

Professor Rashad, a contemporary Afghan historian, explains the the story as follows:

On her way to Afghanistan, Shah Khanum Sultan's caravan reached the Attock River and just before crossing the AttockBridge, Shah Khanum Sultan asked for a break, saying that the journey had been very long and she was very tired. The leader of the caravan accepted her request because he imagined that an unarmed woman couldn't do any harm to anyone. But to his biggest surprise, she suddenly threw herself off the camel, like an eagle into the roaring waves of the Attock River. Babur's soldiers were astonished to see a drowning woman with a happy smile on her face; shouting, "I prefer death with freedom rather than dying in captivity."

Thus, Shah Khanum Sultan became a symbol for all freedom loving women, during the reign of King Babur.

Shah Buri or Shah Pari (Dari)

Shah Pari was a brave and courageous woman. When Babur's troops attacked her village, alone from inside her home, she started fighting against Babur's troops. Never missing a shot, she targeted Babur's soldiers one after another, continuously killing and wounding them. The head of the army officer thought that a large number of skilled fighters were stationed inside the house, so he ordered the house to be surrounded on all sides and targeted it with heavy arrows. The soldiers attacked from all sides and continued the ambush until the firing stopped. Everyone cautiously entered the house to see how many men they had fought against. But when they entered, they were surprised to find that a woman with a perforated body had fallen to the ground. Then they knew that there was only one woman fighting against all the fighting men.

When Babur learned of this story, he was saddened by Shah Buri's death and deeply moved by her bravery. From then on, whenever her name was mentioned, Babur mentioned her name with great admiration, and because of her, he respected and gave special protection to the clan of Amarkhail, who was from the tribe of Shah Buri.

Bibi Mubaraka (The Blessed Queen)

On a trip from Kabul to Ghazni, Emperor Babur learned about a very gentle, extremely beautiful and poised young lady from a noble background by the nameRuqayyah Begum. She was from the Yusufzai tribe. Impressed and interested, he decided to marry her. After the wedding, he named the new queen Bibi Mobaraka (The Blessed One).

When Bibi Mobaraka came to Kabul, she was also fascinated by the charming gardens, inviting atmosphere, and historic background of Kabul. So, she asked Emperor Babur to build a beautiful garden that would be a women's promenade and would add to the beautification of Kabul. Babar accepted her request and invited the best gardeners and architects to build a garden with the most beautiful design, alleyways with ornamental trees, fruit gardens and a large pool surrounded with beautiful flowers and decorative plants. Apparently, all these decisions were made by Queen Mobaraka.

Babur Garden, being built, from Tuzuk Baburi, Kabul, 17th century

During the construction, Queen Mobaraka asked several artists to draw the staff working on the garden. These fine detailed paintings still exist in *TuzukBaburi*, King Babur's Memoirs.

Bibi Mobaraka and her companions were enjoying the beauty of the gardens, especially the pond surrounded by fruit trees and beautiful, charming flowers. Queen Mobaraka also wanted to increase the number of trees, shrubs and flowers for the enjoyment of visitors who would come from distant places to see the Garden. At the entrance of the garden, she ordered the construction of a large Caravanserai, (Guest House). This large building that still exists in Kabul had many   rooms for travelers and visitors.

A View of Babur's Garden in Kabul, built in the17th century AD

When Babur's government was more established, Bibi Mobaraka went to India at the request of Babar. She spent some time in Agra. Deep in her heart she always missed Kabul, so she returned to Kabul after spending only a few months in India. Babar would also visit Kabul frequently, especially on special occasions so that he could participate in horse races in the field near the Citadel of Bala Hessar, the residential palace of Bibi Mobaraka. This was his usual pastime until his old age.

After Babur's death, serious confrontations began between his two sons Homayoun and Kamran. Homayoun went to Persia to seek assistance from the Safavids, and Kamran remained in Delhi. Their disagreements gave a chance to Farid Khan, known as Shirshah Suri, another Afghan ruler to gain control of India.

Despite the political turmoil in India, Bibi Mobaraka wanted to honor her husband's wish and transport him from Agra to Kabul for burial services. Contrary to her close friends' advice against travel to India during such a hostile time, she decided to travel anyway. For this plan, she requested an appointment with Shirshah Suri. Although Shirshah Suri was against Babur's descendants, Bibi Mubarak, a determined woman, did not give up and went ahead with her plans to see Shirshah Suri. Contrary to all expectations, King Shirshah welcomed Bibi Mobaraka with great respect and promised to assist her in achieving her goal. Thus, Shirshah facilitated the transportation of her husband's body to Kabul with the appropriate dignified ceremony accorded to an emperor. He designated a special army to take Babur's body to Kabul with utmost pageantry and splendor. Upon arrival in Kabul, the queen ordered that he be buried in Babur's garden, the burial site he himself had chosen. Bibi Mobaraka did not want any dome on Babar's tomb since she knew that her late husband loved the open air and the clear and starry sky of Kabul nights; a dome would have obstructed the sky view.

Babur's Tomb and the Marble Mosque in Babur's Garden

Threrfore, mausoleum, doesn't have a ceiling, but surrounded only by a delicate marble fence with a stunning artistic beauty.

Bibi Mobaraka lived in Kabul for the rest of her life and was happy to live with the memories of her beloved husband. Visits added to her joy whenever she would visit her husband's charming garden; its tranquil atmosphere, colorful surroundings, and running streams of water gave her the peace of mind she needed.

At her request, she was buried in the same garden, next to her husband after she died.

Ladies of Kandahar

During the reign of Babur and his descendants, the city of Kandahar was an advanced cultural center, where many thinkers, poets, and classical music admirers exchanged ideas. Both Pashto and Dari literature were common in Kandahar during the 17th century.

Classical mystical music in particular had many fans. The pilgrimage to Hassan Abdal's shrine, nicknamed as *Baba Wali*, was a common practice among people of Kandahar. He was a spiritual man that Timurid princes also had high regards for. The Timurid dynasty had a special interest in the beautiful city of Kandahar. *ChilZeena* ("Forty steps") is a mountainous outcrop at the western limit of the city, which was built as a promenade place on the mountain top.

The Monument of Chel Zina and its Elevated Hall

This impressive monument was built by the order of King Babur. The beautiful view of Kandahar gardens can be seen from this vantage point. It is said that Prince Daniel, Prince Askari and Prince Kamran enjoyed musical performances there, especially on moonlit nights and one night belonged to the women of the Babar family.Kandahari women poets of this era would write their poems in both Dari and Pashto languages.

Mirmon Rabia

She was a revered poetess of this era who wrote in Pashto. She had her own realization about the concept of creation. In one of her poems, she talks about the blazing fire that separated the earth from its source and brought about the notion of detachment that mankind still suffers from.

Zarghuna Kakar

Zarghona Kakar, a highly educated woman, lived in the town of Panjwai in Kandahar. She was a talented poetess and a good calligrapher. Zarghuna was involved in studying classical poetry and reading the books of prominent authors. Her father, Din Mohammad Khan Kakar, was a well-read man who encouraged and advised her to read books that would enhance herknowledge. Zarghuna mastered different styles of calligraphy and wrote children's books in Pashto in a poetic form. Her writings were usually inspired by the work of Sa'di, the prominent 8th century Persian Poet. The collection of her poems is still admired by many people, because of its simple style and focus on the subject of morality. Zarghuna's husband, Sadullah Khan Noorzai, was an accomplished scholar. Their children were all interested in education, and as they grew up, they became virtuous and worthy members of the society.

Queen Nur Jahan

Born in the historic city of Kandahar in 1577 AD, Queen Nur Jahan is the most famous and celebrated lady of the 17th century. Her birth name was Mehr-un-Nissa,

but later when she became the powerful queen of India, she received the title of Nur Jahan Begum, (The Light of the World.)

Mehrun-nisa was the daughter of Mirza Ghiasuddin Beg, Etemad al-Dawla, who was a government official. Her mother Esmat Khanum was a well-read lady who had a great interest in Dari literature. Mehrun-nisa spent her childhood and adolescence in the city of Kandahar, where she benefited from association with scholars and became acquainted with different styles of writing poetry. At the age of 17, she traveled to India with her parents and settled in Agra, near Delhi. This was the time that great changes were taking place in her life. She was at the zenith of her charm and beauty during this period of her life in India. It's said that a powerful man named Sher Afgan, also known as Sher Afgan, saw her with her mother while they were shopping. Shir Afgan, madly fell in love with her at first sight, and after a short while, he found an opportunity to meet with her father, Etmad-al Dawla. Sher Afganrespectfully proposed to ask him for her hand in marriage. Shir Afghan had great wealth and prestige that couldn't be ignored. Thus, the father happily agreed to their marriage, without asking his daughter's opinion. When Mehrun-nisa found out about the arranged marriage, she became very upset but out of respect accepted her father's decision.

Shir Afghan, on the other hand, was a politician and a military man, unlike Mehrun-nisa, who had a great interest in poetry, music and dancing. When Shir Afghan was appointed as the governor of Bengal, Mehrun-nisa stayed in Delhi. It is said that during the celebration of Nowruz (New Year) in Emperor Akbar's palace, Mehrun-nisa and her parents were among the royal guests. This is when her dazzling beauty caught Prince Salim's attention, and he madly fell in love with her. For this reason, some people mistakenly think that Nur Jahan is the famous Anarkali, a beautiful singer and dancer that Prince Salim loved. (Anarkali is a fictional character in the popular Indian movie Mughal Azam, and doesn't have any historical reality.)

Obviously, Emperor Akbar was not very happy that his favorite son had fallen in love with a married woman. However, the course of events turned in favor of Prince Salim when Shir Afgan was killed during a battle in Bengal. Now, the time was right for Prince Salim to marry MehrunNisa.

After Emperor Akbar died in 1605, Prince Salim ascended the throne as Emperor Jahangir. In 1611, he married Mehrun-Nisa and gave her the title of Queen Nur Jahan Begum (The Light of the World).

Emperor Jahangir was a man of poetry, music, art and literature; however, due to his excessive habit of drinking, he couldn't perform the duties of a ruler quite well. He spent most of his time, drinking wine; listening to music; writing his memoirs (*TuzukJahangiri*); and writing romantic poems for Nur Jahan. He was fond of playing chess and throwing royal feasts with dancing and musical performances. Since he was not performing the royal duties as expected, Nur Jahan had to take care of all important administrative tasks and make executive decisions.

The emperor's increasing heavy drinking habit added to Nur Jahan's governmental, administrative responsibilities. In reality, she was the real leader of India since Jahangir was lost in his own world. She was making important decisions on Jahangeer's behalf, ranging from major political decisions to financial, administrative, taxation and military affairs. During her reign of the vast territory of the Indian subcontinent, her father and her brother, Abdul Asef Kandahari, would also assist in financial and administrative tasks. Their involvement in these affairs contributed to her family's enhanced power.

At nights when Nur Jahan would come to the Emperor's private chamber from work, Jahangir would be reading her the poems that he had written. His expectation was that Nur Jahan would respond back with her own verses. To the king's great astonishment and admiration, Nur Jahan's had achieved superiority in writing poetry. She was usually more eloquent than any resident poet of his court. Nur Jahan was a naturally born poet. She could answer any poet simultaneously and immediately with utmost eloquence and best choice of lexical and poetic expressions. Thus, Nur Jahan became an idol in the eyes of Emperor Jahangir.

Jahangir passed away in October of 1627. After his death, Nur Jahan ruled the country with wisdom and promoted all forms of art including classical music. She liked beautiful fabrics, which contributed to the growth of the textile industry during her reign. She died in December of 1645 in Lahore at the age of 68. Her grave site is situated next to a train station. Visitors report that for political reasons the site is not very well maintained by the Government of Pakistan, but her memories and her poems are always remembered by her fans.

A view of Taj Mahal in Agra

Queen Momtaz Mahal

Momtaz Mahal was the beautiful wife of Shah Jahan, Jahangir's son, and Queen Nur Jahan's niece. Her father Abdul Hassan Asef Khan, brother of Queen Noor Jahan, was one of the richest men of his time. He named his beloved daughter, Arjumand Begum, (a highly loved and respected lady) and raised her to receive the best education possible in addition to all the comforts that he provided for her as a caring father.

Portriat of Momtaz Mahal

Arjmand Begum frequently visited her powerful aunt at the Royal Palace of Agra, where she became acquainted with Prince Khoram, Jahamgir's Crown Prince. Her poised and polite character, plus her exceptional beauty, made Prince Khoram to like her and propose marriage to her. In 1612 AD, at the age of 19, Prince Khoram married her.Prince Khoram who recived the titile of Shah Jahan was deeply in love with her. Arjmand Begum's warmth and charming personality brought such a joy and pleasant atmosphere to the royal palace that she received the title of Momtaz Mahal (the exalted one of the palace). She was highly respected as the future Queen of a large empire by all the people who knew her. Momtaz Mahal gave birth to several children from this marriage. After 19 years of marriage to Shah Jahan, she passed away in 1631. Shah Jahan was so upset by her death, that he built the grand building of Taj Mahal, in her memory, which is one of the Seven Wonders of the World.

Kandahari Begum

Kandahari Begum was the first wife of Shah Jahan and was a very religious and fateful woman. After the death of Shah Jahan, she became a very powerful lady. She was the sister of Aurangzeb, the great emperor of India. However, in contrast to Aurangzeb's harshness and tyranny, KandahariBegum was a much more considerate and prudent politician. Her goal was to balance the harsh governance of her brother. Although Aurangzeb was a fanatical and strict man, Kandahari Begum was trying to maintain a balanced relationship with the non-Muslim population of India.

Author's Note:

Despite the fact that these influential women played important roles in the cultural and political history of India, either most of them were born and raised in the city of Kandahar or their parents came from Afghanistan.

In this study, the second half of the seventeenth century is important, since it corresponds with the emergence of women poets and authors, in both Pashto and Dari languages. Most of these women, in addition to being well-educated and very knowledgeable, stood against aggression.

Bibi Shamsu

Bibi Shamsu was a talented woman who wrote eloquently, was fiercely independent, and expressed her ideas courageously. She was the daughter of Sheikh Hassan Kaka, the brother of Bayazid Ansari, nicknamed Pir -e -Roshan. Shamsu lived in the Swat and Mohmand areas during the Aurangzeb campaigns. She was a follower of the Pir-e Roshan's movement who was a freedom-loving thinker. Shamsu joined his movement since she couldn't tolerate any prejudice against women. She also stood for enlightenment and struggled against ignorance and oppression. Shamsu liked Bayazid Ansari's ideology, which was based on integrity and protecting of human rights, including women's rights. As her revolutionary poems were becoming more popular, the chance of her arrest increased. Aware of the danger, Shamsu escaped to Kandahar when Aourangseb's military attacks began in the Sawat and Mohmand areas.

She continued to express her views in the form of lyrics and short verses (Pashto Landy. During this period Shamsu did not stay in one city for too long since she knew she would receive harsh punishment if caught. Thus, she would split her time between Ghazni and Gardiz. As a freedom-loving woman, she continued writing although not many examples of her poems have survived. Due to male dominance in the society of the time, no biography of hers has been written independently except for some sketchy information on her life which is contained in "Bayazid Rohan Biography" by Ali Mohammad Mokhles, (contemporary poet in Dari and Pashto

Bibi Nikbakhta

Nikbakhta was the daughter of Sheik Allah Dad Mamozi, a religious scholar. She was greatly inclined towards Sufism. She studied renowned mystic poets, which contributed to the depth of her research and made her one of the most famous poetesses in Pashto.

Under her father's guidance, she also studied theology and subsequently wrote the book of *Irshad al-Foqara* (The Advice of the Sufis) in Pashto. In it she discusses her views on how mystical advice can guide society towards goodness. Her book in particular attracted the young scholars of her time.

Circa 1645, Bibi Nikbakhta married Sheikh Quds Allah, who appreciated her talent, was supportive of her activities, and respected her as a thinker and an eloquent poetess.

Halima Khatak

Halima Khatak was another talented young poetess of this era. She had a unique writing style of her own. As an investigative and critical thinker, she posed questions about life and tried to answer them analytically.

In her two-thousand verse book, Dewan Halima Khatak, she expresses her thoughts and research findings in the form of poetry.

Halima Khattak is considered to have been very innovative in her approach to guiding her readers in the acquisition of knowledge. Like Bibi Nikbakhta, she expresses her thoughts on achieving sublime morality and introducing the ultimate eternal love of the Divine by Praising the Creator of Life and Universe.

Resources

Professor Abdul Ra'uf Benawa (Pashtun Women) Pashto Society Kabul

Masuma Esmati Wardak (Role and Position of Women in Afghanistan)
ProfessorHabibulahTegaythe Pashtun Ladies, Kabul Unversity Press.
Professor A. Habibi,*Pata Khazana,*(The Hidden Treasures of Pashto Literature.) Afghan Minstery of Education Publication.
Prof. Abdul Hai Habibi *Zahiruddin Muhammad Babur*, Baihaqi Publication, Kabul
 Researcher Abdul Rahim Bakhtani, (The Role of Women in the Affairs of the State)
Professor Abdul Ra'uf Benawa (Pashtun Women) Pashto Society Kabul
Masuma Esmati Wardak (Role and position of women in Afghanistan)
Pashto Society, Center for Languages and Literature, Academy of Sciences of Afghanistan
Banks Findley, Ellison (1993). Nur Jahan: Empress of Mughal India. Oxford, UK: Nur Jahan
Memoirs of Jahangir, Emperor of India. Translated by Thackston, Wheeler M. Oxford University Press.

CHAPTER TEN

Afghan Women in the eighteenth Century

In the eighteenth century, Afghan women became more involved in politics, as well as poetry and literature.

Nazo Anna

Nazo Anna, also known as NazoTokhi, was a courageous and intelligent lady from Kandahar. Due to her caring personality and life-long struggle to free Afghanistan from the Persian Safavids' rule, she gained the endearing title of Anna, meaning the Grand Mother.

She was the mother of Mirwais Khan Hotak, the leader who started Afghanistan's independence movement against the Safavids of Persia.

Nazo Anna helped and guided her son to stand for Afghanistan's sovereignty and expel the foreign forces from her country. In the history of Afghanistan, she is remembered not only as a talented poetess and writer but also as a brave woman who struggled for the cause of freedom and justice.

Nazo was the daughter of Sultan MalakhiTokhi, from the city of Qalat, Zabul province. She was born in 1650 in Qalat and spent her childhood and adolescence in Zabul. She was still young when her father was killed in a tribal feud. This horrific incident shook Nazo's life at the age of 16, but she was fortunate to be looked after by her older brother, Adel Khan who, in his late twenties, had to fight to defend his family's honor.

Nazo was very upset to see her brother be involved and away from home for long periods of time on tribal feuds. However, she felt proud that her brother gave her the responsibility to protect their family castle. Adel Khan also provided some guns and ammunition for her for the protection of their village. Like a courageous soldier, Nazo proudly accepted the responsibility and guarded her people. She took the job seriously and as a young leader performed important social, military, and tribal duties. Despite facing adversity and threats, she defended her village, becoming a leader at a very young age. As a military leader, she was well acquainted with the techniques of battle and would make the right decisions in crucial moments. Nazo was dealing with social affairs during this hostile time, and since she gained the respect of the people, she was able to resolve disputes among families. Usually, the local people respected her unbiased opinions, thus her decisions were mostly accepted.

After many months, Adel Khan returned to his village with the good news of peace between the adversarial tribes. The knowledge that his sister had become a brave and successful leader in the community added even more to his joy and pride. Soon Nazo's reputation for justice, courage, and hospitality became well-known from Zabul to Kandahar. For many, her words and deeds actually became examples and symbols of justice, wisdom, and bravery.

At this time, Shah Alam Khan Hottak was a famous leader of Zabul Province. He was an important man, but did not hide the fact that he was very impressed by Nazo and wanted to marry her. He proposed marriage with great respect to Nazo and her entire clan. Being aware of Shah Alam Khan's honesty, integrity and bravery, she accepted to marry him. From this happy marriage, Nazo gave birth to a healthy child that was named MirwaisHottak, who later became the liberator and national leader of Afghanistan.

As Mirwais was growing up, the political situation of Afghanistan was at its worst; on the one hand the cruelties of the Mugal kings of India had reached their peak and on the other hand, the Safavids of Persia had occupied Herat and Kandahar. Nazo knew that for Afghanistan to be independent again, it needed a national leader to repel the Safavids of Persia from Herat and Kandahar and stop the aggression of Aurangzeb's descendants. Thus, she decided to raise her son with all the qualities of a young national leader. Being a practical lady, Nazo Anna would always tell her son:

God created you to do great things. Walk in the right path to remain correct and honest; do not be afraid of anyone or anything. The only thing you should be afraid of is when you are captured by your greed and selfishness. Help the oppressed people who depend on you. And you should always depend on Almighty God and your own merits. God's mercy is unlimited. So, save your homeland from looters, aggressors, and occupiers, so God will be pleased and save your life. Remember this is your national duty.

After Nazo's husband's death and when Mirwais grew up as a strong young man, she and her son moved to Kandahar. They settled in the city of Kandahar where Gorgin, the Safavid Governor, ruled with an iron fist and many people suffered from his atrocities. Hundreds of free thinkers and patriotic people were jailed, tortured and executed mercilessly. After meeting with the leaders of Kandahar about Gorgin's inhuman treatment of their people, Nazo and her son, Mirwais, chose the Garden of Kokaran in the Western outskirts of the city as their base of resistance.

Like his father, Shah Alam Khan Hottak, Mirwais was a tall, handsome and brave man. He had become an eloquent speaker and a smart young man, heavily influenced by his erudite mother about being an efficient and just leader.

Soon under Nazo Anna and her son's leadership, thousands of freedoms loving people who opposed the Safavids domination in Afghanistan gathered around them. They were coming from all walks of life and different Afghan tribes, such as Pashtoons, Uzbeks, Tajiks, Hazaras, Turkmans, and Baluoches. They had one common goal and that was to free their homeland from foreign occupation. Circa 1709, Nazo Anna assured her son that they had sufficient forces that could challenge the Safavid government. Thus, MirwaisHottak publicly denounced Shah Hossein

Portriat of Mirwise Khan

Safavid's rule in Afghanistan. Subsequently, Gurgin, the Safavid governor of Kandahar, was killed during the uprising, and then Persian forces were expelled from Afghanistan.

Mirwais Khan's talent for leadership and good behavior that led him to the rank of libertarian leader comes from his mother. Mirwais was such a graceful orator from a young age. People were impressed by his logic and knowledge, which shows his mother's devotion to teaching him religious studies, history, ethics and political issues from the age of seven. Nazo Anna respected her son from childhood and this is why he was respectful towards others. In fact, MirwisHottak's success in the nation was primarily due to his mother's proper upbringing.

In the year 1710 during the Grand National Assembly (Loya Jirga) in Kokaran Garden, Nazo Anna, in tears of happiness, watched her son giving his historical speech on Afghanistan's independence. His speech was so moving that the leaders of the community suggested that he be the next king of Afghanistan. However, Mirwais Khan didn't accept the offer and instead recited the following poem that he wrote in Dari:

I didn't serve my people to become a king
Or sit on a thrown and wear a crown
I neither want the glory of being a Sultan
Nor the pleasure of possessing gold and silver
I'll be proud to be accepted as the servant of my people
Or one day, would be called the father of the Nation

Contemporary American writer StevenOtfinoskicomments:
This speech was delivered in Kandahar circa 1710, a half a century before the French Revelation, 1789 and Declaration of Independence of the United States of America in 1774. In the era that most countries of the world were controlled by absolute monarchies, Mirwais Khan's speech was very advanced in terms of its democratic nature.

Subsequently, the remainder of the Persian Army was driven out of Afghanistan as planned by Nozo Anna and executed by her brave son, MirwaisHottak. Nazo Anna remained as an advisor and supporter of his son as he was uniting the country with justice. She was not only a woman built for leadership, but she was also an excellent poetess in the Pashto language.

Dew drops from an early dawn narcissus
As tear drops from a melancholy eye
O beauty, I asked, what makes you cry?
Life is too short for me, it answered,
My beauty blooms and withers in a moment,
As a smile which comes and forever fades

This poem, which is written with delicate woman sentiments, became a source of inspiration for future prominent poets such Iqbal Lahori.

To Nazo Anna's great sadness, her brave son, Mirwais, after seven years of hard work passed away in the year 1717. This incident was the biggest blow in her life. She tried her best to serve the nation until her death. The mother and son are both buried in the Garden of Kokaran. Nazo Anna is still remembered as a lady who loved heer country, and also as an eloquent poetess in Pashto language.

Zainab Hotaki

Zainab Hotaki was the very talented and intelligent daughter of Mirwais Khan Hotak, who was raised by her erudite grandmother, Nazo Anna. Zainab wrote excellent poetry and learned to serve others from her grandmother. Zainab had two brothers, Shah Mahmud Hottaki, who invaded Persia and ended the Safavid dynasty in 1725. Her other brother, Shah Hussain Hottaki ruled Afghanistan from 1720 to 1738. He built a charming citadel, in the Capital city of Kandahar, called the Narenj Palace (Orange Palace). Shah Hussian had great interest in both Pashto and Dari literature and made his court the meeting place of poets, writers and scholars. Sometimes Zainab, along with other women poets, went to Orange Palace. Shah Hussian had always reserved a special chamber for women to follow the poetic and scholarly discussions from their chamber, which was separated from the main hall by beautiful curtains.

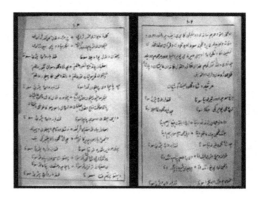

Zainab Poem in HerOwn Handwriting,
Early 18th Century Afghanistan National Archive

It is said that Zainab also established a center for women poets in the outskirts of Kandahar. Women of Kandahar came from nearby and far away places to meet with her. Zeinab Hotaki held literary gatherings where ladies would recite their poems and exchange ideas. Zainab's poems were mostly about morality, ethics, and Sufism. Zainab's teacher and mentor, Mullah Noor Mohammad Gheljai, was a famous scholar in Islamic studies and Sufism who taught mystical literature to Zainab and many other students.

One day, while carrying on her cultural activities, a sudden, very unfortunate incident shook her life, the untimely and mysterious death of her young brother Mahmud Hotaki in Isfahan. He was the conqueror of Persia and had many enemies in Persia. While mourning her brother's death and devastated by the news, Zainab wrote a sorrowful eulogy, which most Pashto literary critics consider as one of the literary masterpieces in the Pashto language.

Mirmon Gulnara

During this hostile time, far from the king's palaces and away from the hustle and bustle of the city life, lived a free spirited woman named Gulnara. People called her Mirmon Gulnara, (Mrs. Gulnara.) She belonged to an Afghan Kuchi (nomadic) tribe and was popular for composing expressive short poems that people loved.

A Quiet Night with the Afghan Nomads

In historic records on Pashto folkloric poetry, her father's name has been mentioned as Suleiman, who was a brave and strong Kochi tribesman. It is said that Gulnara was a very beautiful, courageous and outspoken woman. She was not literate, but other people recorded her rhythmic lyrics that singers loved to sing. Her loving soul expressed the love of God and nature.

Despite their simplicity, her lyrics sometimes conveyed deep symbolic meanings. Her style was simple, fluent, and to the point. They were descriptive of Kuchi life, their people, their animals, and their travels in different places. While traveling through deserts, pasture, farmlands, and mountains, Gulnara described the beauty of nature, especially the tulips and undomesticated flowers. In her short lyrics, she illustrated what she saw and felt quite effectively.

The short rhythmic verses in Pashto are called *Landai*, a form of Pashto folk poetry. Prominent Pashto literature scholars and researchers attribute the writing of this form of poetry to women.

Some critics believe that Gulnara was a follower and admirer of Bibi Shamsu because of her freedom loving nature, but there is no sufficient evidence to prove this. However, Gulnara expressed herself in the most realistic and honest manner.

Refrences

Dupree, Louis (1980). Afghanistan. Princeton University Press

Malleson, George Bruce (1878). History of Afghanistan, from the Earliest Period to the Outbreak of the War of 1878. London

Ewans, Martin; Sir Martin Ewans (2002). Afghanistan: a short history of its people and politics. New York: Perennial

Otfinoski, Steven (2004). Afghanistan. Infobase Publishing.

Anjuman-iTārīkh-iAfghānistān (1967). Afghanistan, Volumes 20-22. Historical Society of Afghanistan.

Hōtak, Muhammad; ʿAbd al-ḤayyḤabībī; Khushal Habibi (1997). Patakhazana. United States,

Malleson, George Bruce (1879) History of Afghanistan, from the Earliest Period to the Outbreak of the War of 1878 W.H. Allen & Co., London

CHAPTER ELEVEN

Afghan Women of the Durrani Empire

Zarghuna Anna

In the year 1737, Nader Afshar of Persia attacked Herat, but he faced strong resistance by the Afghans, led by Zulfiqar Khan, the son of Mohammad Zaman Khan Abdali and Zarghuna Anna. However, the continued strong artillery attacks of Nader Afshar on the city of Herat weakened the Hotaki dynasty's rule to a great extent. At this difficult time, Zarghuna rose as an important political figurehead.

She was the daughter of Khaloo Khan Alokozai, an influential personality who lived in Herat and mother of Zulfiqar Khan, the leader of the arm resistance against Nadir Afshar. She was a freedom-loving and resourceful woman, to whom people looked up during this hostile time.

As the aggression of Nadir Afshar increased on the city of Herat, Zarghuna went to Kandahar to meet in person with Shah HussianHotaki to warn him about the grave situation of the country. On this trip both of her sons, Zulfiqar Khan Abdali and Ahmad Khan Abdali (Ahmad Shah Durrani), accompanied their mother. However, Shah Hussain Hotaki, who was a highly cultured king, but not a prudent politician, feared Zurguna Anna and her son's popularity and influence. He thought that Zarghuna Anna and her son Zulifiqar might topple his government with the backing of powerful Durrani and Abdali tribes. Thus, upon recommendation of some of his advisers, he imprisoned them. This wrong decision gave a perfect opportunity for Nadir Afshar to capture Herat and marched towards Kandahar.

As a result of Nadir Afshar's heavy artillery attacks which lasted for several days, the historic city of *Zor Shar* (Old Town Kandahar) was leveled to ground and the Hotaki dynasty's strong kingdom ended in 1737.

Nadir Afshar, on the other hand, who was aware of Zarghuna Anna and her son's popularity did not kill them, but sent them, along with a large number of influential Afghan personalities to the daunting jail of Mazandaran, in northwest present-dayIran.Zarghuna and her sons spent the worst days of their lives in the Mazandaran prison. She was especially devastated after she discovered that her brave elder son,

Zulifqar, was poisoned and killed. However, she did not give up hope and instead tried to instill in her younger son Ahmad Khan Abdali leadership attributes. Her hope was that upon release from the prison, Ahamad Khan would have all the qualifications to become a strong leader and would make Afghanistan a mighty independent state again.

Among the Afghan detainees, according to the prominent Afghan historian Ghobar, other important leaders like Mir Hotak Afghan also had similar goals for an independent Afghanistan. With her influential personality and extraordinary political savvy, while still in jail, Zargunna Anna created a secret circle of resistance. Simultaneously, inside Afghanistan the resistance against Nader Afshar was growing in major cities such as Herat, Kabul, Balkh and Kandahar. Encountering such resistance, Nadir Afshar had to compromise with the Afghan local leaders in order to maintain his power. After getting some local support, Nadir Afshar decided to invade India. As a politician, he knew that without the support of the Afghans, he would not be successful to conquer India.

When Zarghuna learned about this new development, while still in prison, shewrote a litterto NadiAfshar and explained that under the leadership of Ahmad Khan Abdali and Mir Hotak Afghan, a strong Afghan Army can be established to serve the purpose. Afshar accepted her proposal since he was aware of their political influence in Afghanistan. Subsequently, Ahmad Khan Abdali became the head of Afghan Platoon in Nader Afshar's Army. Due to Ahmad shah's bravery and exceptional military skills, Nader Afshar was able to conquer Delhi in 1739. After the conquest of India, Nidir Afshar confiscated all the royal treasures of the Mughal Empire, including the *Peacock Throne* and the famous *Koh-e Noor* Diamond.

On the way back to Persia, Afshar had his harem and the most expensive treasure of the world with him. He was very watchful so as to protect the caravan from being attacked. He trusted Afghans the most, among whom Ahmad Khan and his men were members of this grand caravan. Upon his mother's recommendation, Ahmad Khan was spending his time reading history and poetry books as well as political manuscripts during this time throughout these travels.

Nadir Afshar became more and more brutal as a result of his greed and his desire to extort more taxes on his subjects. These actions caused his army to revolt against him. He was killed in 1747 on the way to Persia. The Persian and Kurdish troops decided to loot his treasures and dishonor his harem, but Ahmad Khan Abdali, obligated by the Afghan Code of Honor, saved his wife and children and safely brought them to Mashhad, in northe east Iran and gave them amnesty under his protection. In return, Nadir Shah Afshar's wife gave him the Koh-e Noor Diamond as a token of her appreciation.

After Nadir Afshar's death, a power vacuum was created in the country which needed to be filled. Thus, the Afghan leaders convened a Loya Jirga in Kandahar to elect a leader for Afghanistan. In the historic Loya Jirga of Kandahar, Ahmad Shah Durrani was elected as the new leader of Afghanistan, in July 1748.

Coronation of Ahmad Shah Durrani in Loya Jirga of Kandahar

Zurghuna Anna's dream for the creation of an independent, powerful Afghanistan was realized. Ahmad Shah gained the title of Dur-e Duran, circa, 1748 and under his leadership, the mighty Durrani Empire was established, extending from Delhi to Mashhad and Nishapur or Neyshabur.

Zarghuna Anna encouraged her son to develop the country and promote education. During Ahamad Shah's reign, schools adjacent to mosques were established across the country. Zarghuna Anna continued very actively in bringing peace and order in the country. She knew how to keep the public calm in chaotic situations. It is reported that when she heard the rumor about her son's death in the war, she did not lose her temperament and instead tried to calm the public. She addressed the distressed people of Kandahar in a loud and confident voice:

My son Ahmad Shah is not someone who retreats in the war and turns his back on the enemy. If he has been martyred in service of his homeland, he will be blessed as a national hero. But this country does not belong to him alone. If Ahmad Shah is not alive anymore, it would be your responsibility to defend and serve your country. So, do not let anxiety govern your hearts. I am sure that he is alive, and he will come back to serve his people.

Zarghuna Anna believed that her son should treat all the inhabitants of Afghanistan fairly and equally. It is said that when Ahmad Shah Durrani decided to build a wall around the city of Kandahar, Zarghuna Anna stopped him and said, "My son, a ruler of this big nation should never separate himself from the rest of the country behind the walls of Kandahar.

Ahmad Shah abandoned the construction of the rest of the wall, limiting the construction to just building a military fort and artillery barracks. That's why, like other kings, he did not build a royal palace for himself. He lived in his father's house in Achakzai Alley until his death.

Ahmad Shah Durrani was an accomplished poet in both Dari and Pashto languages. In his Dari poetry book there is a poem that he wrote upon Zarghuna Anna's advice; a couplet from the poem reads as follows:

I feel sorry for the Amir who doesn't care for his people
And, alas, the oppressed leave his door unhappily

Zarghuna Anna is still fondly remembered by Afghans. One of the famous girls' high schools in Kabul is named after her as Zarghuna High School.

The Tomb of Zarghona Ana

Aliah Sultana, wife of Ahmad Shah Durrani

A benevolent lady, Queen Alia Sultana was the daughter of Suleiman Khan Kayani, one of the survivors of ZaranjMalukMehrabani (the Kindness Kings). The young queen followed the path of her benevolent ancestors. In her biography, she is described as an extremely kind and caring lady. She was very helpful and generous who would go out of her way to assist the needy and helpless people.

According to Wakil Popalzai, a contemporary Afghan historian, the mother of Timur Shah, the crown prince was a very influential lady, Timur Shah was appointed as the governor of Herat at a very young age. His mother had to be in charge of the affairs during his youth until the young prince reached the right age to be the governor of an important province. During her stay in Herat, she lived in the historic Fortress of Ikhtiaruddin. To keep the people of Herat happy, she would travel to every corner of the province. Her goal was to see the living condition of the common people and to make sure that people wouldn't face cruelty and injustice by government officials and powerful people.

Bibi Aino

Bibi Aino was an ordinary lady who lived in the city of Kandahar during the reign of Ahmad Shah Durrani. Her good deeds made her famous among the people of Kandahar. Professor Rashad has written a detailed description of Bibi Aino's life and the large property that has been named after her. This large property, which is equipped with an underground irrigation system, is located next to Kabul and Kandahar Highway. Today, in her honor, a beautiful palace, Aino Mina, has been built in this area.

The local Kandahari stories indicate that Aino was a newlywed lady. She was charming and straightforward. Right after her marriage, her husband went to war as a soldier in Ahmad Shah Durrani's army.

One night when Aino was at home, thinking about her husband's safety in the army, she heard a sound in the front yard. She peaked through the window and to her biggest surprise; she realized that her husband was standing in the yard. Aino happily asked if the war was over and her husband had returned home safely.

The husband replied, "No, the war is not over." I was in the camp when I remembered you and since you are very dear to me, I could not bear the thought of not being with you. Aino asked where the other soldiers were. "They are all in the camp including the king himself," replied her husband. Aino became very angry but replied in a calm tone: "I regret that you are so weak and unstable in the performance of your duty while all the other soldiers and officers, including the king himself, are in the army barracks. How can you be so irresponsible? Now go back to the camp and fulfill your duty. Go, go back or I will never see your face again," she exclaimed. When Ahmad Shah Durrani found out about this story, he invited Aino to his office and received her with great respect. In recognition of her patriotism and love of country, he gave her the best piece of land in Kandahar where a whole new region of Kandahar city has now been named after her.

The Newly built Building in Bibi Aino's Property

Fatima Begum, Queen of Timur Shah Durrani

An educated lady, Fatima Begum was Timur Shah Durrani's wife. To assist her husband, she participated in administrative tasks of the country. Her kindness and exceptional, active participation in social affairs won the hearts of many of her compatriots. Intelligent and politically savvy, she often advocated for those who were unjustly condemned to receive harsh punishments. Just like an experienced lawyer, she would protect those who had been unreasonably threatened or unfairly judged. She would carefully listen to people's pleas, serve as a mediator, and give her unbiased opinion to Timur Shah.

She was an enlightened queen who advocated education for women; she would encourage the female visitors to Bala Hisar Palace in Kabul to educate them, to learn, and to grow intellectually. She loved literature and often participated in meetings of poetry readings. The symbolic poems and allegorical style of Mīrzā Abdul-QādirBēdil, a famous, 17th century Dari poet, were very popular in Kabul during this era. Interpreting Bedil's complex ideas was not an easy task; understanding his poetry had become a very popular test of intellectual prowess in Kabul. Interest in Bedil's poetry was high during this era since Timur Shah was very interested in Bedil's writings, too. Queen Fatima was so good at analyzing Bedil's confusing poems that her excellent interpretation and analysis of Bedil's sonnets would most often surprise Timur Shah.Her sense of justice, advocacy for women's education, and her knowledge of literature had won her the respect and admiration of her people, including Timur Shah's brothers', especially Shah Shuja, who was an accomplished poet himself. He had great respect for her and admired her ability to understand and analyze such a complicated style of poetry. Queen Fatima Begum died in the Kabul Bala Hisar fort. Although not very accurate, historical records estimate her date of death between 1793 and 1800 AD.

Zohra Begum, Queen of Shah Zaman

Zohra Begum lived in the late 18th century and the beginning of the 19th century. She was especially interested in building majestic palaces, designing royal gardens, and in the field of literature the Epics of Shahnamah.

The Palace of Jahan Noma, Kabul, Early 19 century

Her biggest dream was to build a splendid palace in the outskirts of Kabul and name it Takht-e Rustam.Zohra Begum wanted to build this splendid palace in Rudaba's honor, since Rudaba, Rustam's mother was born in Kabul and she married Zall Rustam's father in the historic city of Kabul.She proposed her idea to Emperor Shah Zaman who liked her plan. Before the construction work began, she explained to builders her plan, which was a building with a dome in the shape of Rustam's Helmet. The builders agreed to the plan and began the construction.

In studying the palace today, it appears that Queen Zohra's meticulous design specifications are missing in the structure. Also, regarding this matter, Kabul citizens have different opinions, but the great Afghan historian Ahmad Ali Kohzad offers this explanation:

"The western part of the forty-column palace is the same as Takht-e Rustam, which was created by the order of the wife of Shah Zaman, grandson of Ahmad Shah Durrani. Later, during the reign of Amir Abdul Rahman Khan, repairs were made to that building and it became known as Chilsotoon, or the Palace of Forty Pillars."

Loya Adeh

At the beginning of the 19th century the conflicts between Shah Zaman and his brothers on the one hand, and with the Barakzai brothers, the offsprings of Sardar Payendah Mohammad Khan, on the other hand, created chaos in the country. During this politically troubled period, the emergence of some prominent women played important roles in the political relations of Afghanistan with the neighboring countries.One of the most noteworthy, influential, and intelligent women who can be compared to Zarghuna Anna was Loya Ade. Politically intelligent, LoyaAdeh was the courageous mother of Wazir Fateh Khan, an astute politician to whom the British referred as the *King Maker*. His followers had a great deal of respect for him. He and his mother lived at the time that the British were slowly advancing towards Afghanistan, especially after the conquest of Kashmir; LoyaAdeh found the British move alarming. Thus, she encouraged her brave son, Wazir Fateh Khan, to liberate Kashmir from British control. A very experienced military man, Fateh Khan did what his mother had suggested, liberating Kashmir from British rule with a swift military strike.After his brilliant victory in the battle of Kashmir, LoyaAdeh told his son:

Now that you and I have earned the enmity of the British and other enemies of the homeland, we should be very careful in our relations with others, especially those who are powerful and have the throne of Kabul.You know that Russians and the Persians are also on the move towards our homeland.

LoyaAdeh's prediction came to be true since during this time the Russians supported and encouraged the Qajar government of Persia or (Today's Iran) to occupy Herat.

Upon hearing the disturbing news, Fateh Khan rushed to Herat. However, he was deceived by Shah Mahmud and Prince Kamran, who were negatively influenced by the Persians against Fateh Khan. Being proud of his military prowess, Fateh Khan trusted them although this decision was contrary to his mother's advice.

The author of Siraj al-Tawarikh, Faiz Mohammad Katib, in the first volume of his books writes about the enmity of king of Fars towards Wazir Fateh Khan, as follows: "Fath Ali Shah Qajar, who had come to Mashhad, emphasized that in order to resolve the animosity between the two governments, Fateh Khan, who was responsible for the war between Afghanistan and Persia, should be arrested and sent to the court of Persia or should be deprived of sight. "(P. 97)

Thus, following the Persian plan, Prince Kamran captured Fateh Khan while he was unarmed, blinded him in Ghazni, and then killed him in cold blood.

When the devastating news reached LoyaAdeh, the brave woman didn't show any sign of weakness. Instead, she asked the messengers calmly, "Did he shout or moan when he was being blinded?" The messengers replied that no one heard anything.

LoyaAdeh replied, "Then that was my brave son who was defeated by the deception of others. Yes, he was my hero. Alas, he did not listen to his mother's advice."

It is said that when the messenger left, LoyaAdeh shed a few drops of tears and then died silently.

Refrences

Gommans, Jos J. L. (1995). The Rise of the Indo-Afghan Empire: C. 1710-1780. Brill.

Habibi, Abdul Hai. 2003. "Afghanistan: An Abridged History." Fenestra Books

Romano, Amy. "An Historical Atlas of Afghanistan, 2003."

Singh, Ganda (1959). Ahmad Shah Durrani, father of modern Afghanistan. Asia Publishing House,

Singh, Ganda (1959) Ahmad Shah Durrani: Father of Modern Afghanistan Asia Publishing House, London

Singh, Ganda (1959) Ahmad Shah Durrani: Father of Modern Afghanistan Asia Publishing House, London

CHAPTER TWELVE

Afghan Women in the 19th century & During the First Anglo Afghan War

During the reigns of Timur Shah Durrani and his son Shah Zaman, the literary and cultural atmosphere in Kabul had developed greatly. Timur Shah held literary meetings in his palace, and reading Bedil's poetry was a popular pastime in his court. Shah Shuja, Shah Mahmud, and their sons all had poetic talent.

Interest in poetry and literature, especially reading Bedil's philosophical poetry, had also flourished among the common people of Kabul. According to most historians, this literary growth was not limited to men, but most women of this period, both in the Shah's court and in their homes, were very interested in poetry and literature. Even young girls were familiar with Hafez and Omar Khayyam's work. During the reign of Timur Shah, Ayesha Durrani became a famous poet in her young age.

Ayesha Durrani

At this point in time, the literary talent of a young girl, named Ayesha Durrani was noticed by Timur Shah. She was the daughter of Yaqub Ali, an officer of the Royal Army's Artillery Forces. Ayesha, as a young poetes, was well-versed by the poetry lovers in the city of Kabul. Her thoughts were fresh and words vividly expressed her feelings as a young woman.

It is said that when Timur Shah returned to Kabul from a battle, Ayesha wrote a

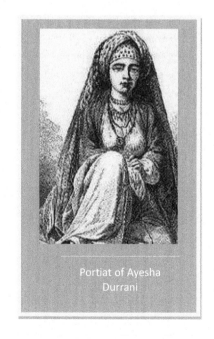

Portiat of Ayesha Durrani

114

touching poem, describing the natural charm and beauty of Kabul.

It was a fine literary piece evocative, of her talent and feelings. Timur Shah was greatly impressed and encouraged Ayesha, since her poetry was different from the general poems of other poets who wrote on the same subject. Her words as a young woman expressed her feminine sentiments while later in life her writing dealt with feelings of motherhood and life's tragic events.

Ayesha Durrani had a normal life until she experienced a devastating incident, the tragic death of her son, Zia-al-Wald, in the battle of Kashmir. He was in his early 20s while serving as a soldier in the artillery unit of Shah Zaman's army. This tragic occurrence made Ayesha to write most melancholy poems about her son's death and express her motherly feelings in condemnation of war as expressed in these verses to Shah Zaman:

I saw the reddest sunset at sunrise
The sunrise of my life became dark as sunset
Perhaps someone has killed the sun
And that's why the skirting of the sky
Is covered with the blood of sinfulness

Using **sun** in this allegorical poem, she is referring to her son and his death since the word Zia means sunlight in Arabic and Dari.

After this incident, Ayesha wrote about the feelings of women who lived inside the walls of the limited atmosphere of the castles and Herams; a world that has been created by men who are engaged in wars to gain power and women had to suffer from it.

Ayesha had a courageous personality and expressed her feelings bravely in the presence of powerful men. Perhaps she was more advanced for her time. Her self-reliance, polite demeanor, and brave strong language made her famous in the court of Shah Zaman and other princes. Historians have divided Ayesha Durrani's literary life into three parts.

A- The first phase is the period of her youth and the beginning of her profession as a poet. She followed the style of Hafez Shirazi and other classical poets to write her poetry. However, she added her own innovative approach to convey her thoughts.

B- Poems that have a social aspect and were written after the death of her young son Zia al Walad, whose loss affected her emotionally. This is the period that she wrote the melancholiest poetry. Like her famous mournful poem -- "Without You!"

C- This is the period of her maturity as a full-fledged, accomplished professional poet. During this phase, she wrote the philosophy of her life; her understanding of living as a human being; and her devotion for the Love of the Divine, in which one can see a mythical tone of Sufism.

Ayesha Durrani's poems were collected by a fine writer named Hashem Khan Shariati. It was published by the Kabul Printing House during the reign of King Abdul Rahman. According to most Afghan scholars, Ayesha Durrani has written 3,000 poems, some of which have been printed.

Although Ayesha Durrani belonged to the Pashtun Durrani people, she wrote her poetry in Dari and never expressed any bias against any other languages or ethnicities. For this reason, the intellectuals and the youth of Afghanistan today call her a*transnational* poet. Ayesha is highly valued and respected in contemporary Afghan poetic circles.

In her honor, one of the first women's schools in Kabul is named after her, *Aisha Durrani Lycee*, famous for graduating well-prepared students for higher education in the country and abroad.

Khadija Begum

Queen Khadija Begum was Amir Dost Mohammad Khan's wife and mother of Prince Akbar Khan, the hero of First Anglo Afghan War. Khadija Begum was born in the old district of Kabul (Chandawal), circa 1792. She was in Kabul when 21,000 British troops equipped with heavy artillery, thousands of camels, and hundreds of elephants entered Afghanistan.

It was the most devastating moment of her life to see her beloved country being attacked by a foreign power. In 1839, the British army entered Kabul and installed Shah Shuja, who was in exile in India, as the puppet king of Afghanistan.

It was difficult for Queen Khadija to bear the sight of a puppet government at a crucial time when her husband, King Dost Mohammad Khan and his son Prince Akbar, had left for Bukhara to seek military assistance against the British from Bukhara's Amir Nasrullah. During this difficult time, to her biggest surprise and dismay, she learned that the Amir of Bukhara had imprisoned her husband and her son. Perhaps

Shah Shuja in the Palace of Bala Hissar

Nasrullah was too afraid to ruin his relationship with such a powerful country as Great Britain.

Thus, Khadija Begum had to play her role as the mother of the nation and struggle for the freedom of Afghanistan. It is said that before Shah Shuja, the puppet king of Great Britain, entered the Palace of Bala Hissar, Khadija Begum voluntarily left the palace. Clearly, she couldn't tolerate the presence of British advisors, like William McNaughton and AlexanderBurns, who were giving Shah Shuja orders on how to govern the country. Moreover, she was furious to see that British general, like Major-General Sir Henry Sale, Lieutenant General Kane, and the most famous of all Major-General George Elphinston, control all the major military bases of Kabul, Jalalabad, Ghazni and Kandahar. While starting a successful resistance movement against the enormous military power of the British was not an easy task, she was determined to expel the British forces from her soil. During this time, she lived in her father's home in downtown Kabul. This was when her sister-in-law,

Portrait of Prince Akbar Khan

nicknamed Madad Khan's Mother, came to see her. She informed her that a serious resistance movement against the British invaders was being formed in Kabul. Therefore, Khadija Begum, along with her equally enthusiastic sister-in-law, met with Mohammad Hussian Khan Chandawali, who was a relative and one of the resistance leaders. During their meeting, she conveyed her full support for the resistance movement. Subsequently, both ladies traveled to the outskirts of Kabul and met with national leaders. Both had respectful relations with most of the national leaders such as Mir Masjedi Khan, Mir Bacha Khan Kohdamani, Abdullah Khan Achakzai, Aminullah Khan Logari, Imam Werdi Khan Mazari, Nawab Zaman Khan, Shuja Dowlla and leaders of Kunar and Paktia. They all assured her that they would fight for the liberation of Afghanistan. All the strong leaders respected her as a kind mother and promised her that they would never disappoint their queen who is the spiritual mother of the nation.

Thus, Khadija Begum had to play her role as the mother of the nation and struggle for the freedom of Afghanistan.

Obviously, starting a successful resistance movement against the enormous military power of the British was not an easy task. The British army had superior weapons and an advanced logistical system which gave them an upper hand in the battles.

At those moments of desperation, the good news of the freedom of Prince Akbar and his father from the prison of Bukhara gave a great morale boost to Khadija Begum

and the entire resistance movement. Everyone knew of Prince Akbar's heroism in the Battle of Jamrud when he defeated the British-backed mighty army of Punjab on April 30, 1837; they all felt that their freedom from prison signified the independence of Afghanistan.

Throughout the nation, people from all walks of life, young and old started an arms resistance against the British army. Subsequently, Sir Alexander Burns, one of the prominent British deplomats was killed during an uprising in Kabul.

According to Lady Sale, wife of General Sale, who was living in Kabul at the time, the Afghan resistance movement was growing stronger and more frightening every day. During the uprising of Kabul, Queen Khadija Begum organized several groups of women to prepare food and medication for the freedom fighters. The two brave ladies traveled to battlefields, and along with other volunteer women, found skilled physicians to treat the soldiers wounded in war.

Prince Akbar prepared a national army consisting of all ethnicities of Afghanistan and challenged the British forces. Major-General George Elphinston, the most celebrated British general who defeated Napoleon Bonaparte in the Battle of Waterloo was the head of the British army. The two armies fought in a section of Kabul which is now called Wazir Akbar Khan District. The British political envoy Sir William McNaughton, who was the main architect of the British invasion of Afghanistan, was killed by Prince Akbar. Then General Elphinston and his forces started to retreat towards Jalalabad. Lady Sale writes in her memoirs:

"The Afghans gave amnesty to British women and children to safely leave their country, but our forces had to fight for their lives in order to leave Afghanistan." [7]

While English families were leaving Afghanistan, the Afghan women were involved in taking care of the wounded. They were working side by side with their fathers, brothers, husband, and neighbors to transport the wounded to safety; homes were utilized as hospitals. It is said that Khadija Begum changed her personal residence to a makeshift hospital despite the fact that she was worried about her son's life who was involved in driving out the British Army on their way to Jalalabad

At last Khadija Begum was relieved to learn that all the British army had left the Afghanistan soil and the only survivor from 21,000 British troops was a man by the name of William Brydon.

After the withdrawal of the British army, Khadija Begum was involved in advising Amir Dost Mohammad Khan on political matters. She was a prudent lady and usually her advice was accurate and truthful. It is said that she played a valuable role in rebuilding bridges and roads that were destroyed during the war. According to the local people of Kabul, one of the bridges to connect the road between Kabul and Paghman was originally built by her, and later restoured by Queen Halima the powerful, wife of King Abdurhaman in the 1880s.

---

[7]Lady Sale's Account of the Retreat from Kabul During the First Afghan War

Legend of Bibi Mahro

Historical archives show most battles of the Afghan Liberation Movement against the British forces took place in the fields between the Shirpour Military Garrison and Bibi Mahro Hill, located near Kabul Airport. There is a fascinating story among the people of Kabul about a young lady called Bibi Mahro that can't be ignored.

It is said that on this hill lived a beautiful girl named Mahro. From there, she watched the war between the Afghan freedom fighters and the British army. The feeling of patriotism boiled in her blood; she couldn't stand seeing her countrymen get killed or wounded by foreign soldiers whose sole goal was to occupy her country. Routinely, she would rush to the aid of Afghan fighters and give them food. She became more active, especially after her beloved fiancée, Aziz, joined the freedom fighters. Thus, Mahro would come more frequently to the battle field with the village girls and help nurse the wounded.

She was courageously involved in helping her countrymen until the night that she heard Aziz had been wounded. It was a dark, gloomy winter night. Mahro started searching for Aziz in the fighting fields. The heavy snow and strong wind prevented her from finding her beloved fiancée among the wounded. She returned home with great sadness and became severely ill with fever and chest pains, shivering and coughing the whole night while thinking about Aziz. She was hoping to hear some good news but died in distress early in the morning.

Despite his severe wounds, Aziz did not die when he returned to the village. When he heard the tragic news about Mahro, he went to her grave, shedding many tears of grief and sorrow. When night fell, the villagers discovered that Aziz had died while grieving for Mahro.

Aziz's family buried him next to his fiancée, and from then on, the hill was referred to as Bi-Mahro Hill and sometimes, the Hill of the Two Lovers.

However, other stories are also told about Bibi Mahro's Hill by Afghan contemporary writers who offer varying accounts of the death of these two lovers:

In the distant past, two influential families, Malik Mir Afghan and Malik Afzal Khan, lived on this hillside. The two clans were hostile towards each other, resulting in family feuds. Mir Afghan had a beautiful daughter, named Mahro. She would take walks around the wheat fields in late afternoons. In one of her walks, she encountered a young man by the name of Aziz who was very poised and polite. After seeing each other during these walks, they fell in love.

Bibi Mahro Hill with the tallest Afghan flag, gifted by the India Government

Mirman Speena

Mirman Speena was the mother of the powerful governor of Herat, Yar Mohammed Khan Alikozai. She was an influential lady who lived in a very critical juncture of Afghan history and played a very important role in the political sovereignty and territorial integrity of Afghanistan.

During the First Anglo Afghan War when the country was in turmoil, with the persuasion of the Russian Tsarist government, the Qajar regime of Persia took advantage of the situation to invade Herat. As a patriotic lady, Mirman Speena talked to her son and advised him that under no circumstances should he allow the Persians or any outsiders advance in the city of Herat. Though the Afghan resistance leaders were still preoccupied with averting the British Army who were preparing for a reprisal attack on Afghanistan's eastern and southern borders, Mirman Speena helped her brave son to protect the western borders of Afghanistan. With the help of his mother, Yar Mohammad Khan managed to organize a strong army to defend Herat.

To persuade the young fighters for Afghanistan's independence, Mirman Speena wrote patriotic poems. Her poems were well received by many Afghans, and her Pashto poems in particular became very popular in Kandahar. It is said that Mirman Speena personally traveled to different localities of Herat and Badghisprovinces to establish a strong army. Because of her appeal as a respected elderly woman, many young fighters joined the resistance movement.

Herat in the 19th century, an illustration from London News

Mirman Speena and her son are considered as the saviors of Herat during the competition between Britain and Russia during the Great Games era in the mid-19th century. Mirman Speena played a vital role as a devoted mother in the most crucial moment of Afghan history. She was a heroine that will always be remembered.

Amena Fedawi

While Mirman Speena played an important role in the politics of this era, Amena Fedawi stood tall in the arena of literature. She was an accomplished poet and calligrapher. Her poems were eloquent, with a touch of Sufism and strong devotion to God.Amena Fedawi was the daughter of Sardar Noor Ahmad Khan, one of the nobilities of this period. On her mother's side, she was related to King Amir Dost Mohammad Khan. Despite her high status in society, she was a very modest and grounded person.

Amena Fedawi was born around 1857 AD in downtown Kabul. Like the rest of the royal families, her parents lived in the luxurious Palace of Bala Hisar, but Amena preferred to live in their humble home in downtown Kabul.

Amena was raised in the heart of the city with its rich cultural environment, learning from the intellectuals, philosophers, calligraphers, and poets, who lived in Old Town Kabul. Old Town Kabul at the foothills of Shir-Darwaza and Asmaie Mountains was a very interesting place to live. Although badly damaged during the First Anglo-Afghan War, it was still a charming town with many gardens, numerous shops, and several streams running through the city. Kabul had many bazaars for specific products where Amena liked to spend her time, particularly in the Book Sellers Street which was considered a dwelling place of poets and the intellectuals. Coming from an affluent family, Amena Fedawi was able to finance the building of mosques and *Khanaqas* (A special building for dervishes and musicians in the worship and praise of the Almighty God). Amena Fedawi was a devout Muslim who performed Hajj two times during her life time. After her return from the first pilgrimage to Mecca, she built the Bagh Ali Mardan Mosque in downtown Kabul. The mosque is still standing and was restored by Afghanistan Historic Monuments Preservation Bureau during Ashraf Gani'stime in office.

Amena Fedawi was a benevolent lady. Not having been married, she spent most of her time and resources on the education of young girls who were eager to learn. It is said that before going to Mecca for the second time, she wanted to spend all her funds on promoting education. She was a disciplined, forward-looking and organized planner. Before embarking on the journey to Mecca, she put aside some money for her trip and bought all the necessary items needed for a burial since her biggest wish was to be buried either in Mecca or in Medina. Her wish, however, didn't come true during her visit to the holy places. However, according to the travelers who were with her on this trip, on the way back from the pilgrimage, she suddenly felt the presence of Bilal Ibn Rabah, the closest disciple of Prophet Mohammad, and smiled with ecstasy. A day later after dinner while traveling through Syria, her bus, carrying the Afghan pilgrims suddenly went off the road, causing the death of only one passenger, and that was Amina. The next morning as the passengers were waiting on the roadside for assistance, a scholar of Jerusalem came to the scene and asked if a woman had died among the Afghan pilgrims. Her companions showed him Amena's body. The man said that he saw Saint Bilal in his dream and that Bilal had ordered him to bury her body next to his grave. For this reason, Amena Fedawi's burial is in Damascus in the complex of Bilal Ibn Rabah's Mausoleum. In her honor and due to her dedication to the promotion of education for women, a girl's high school in Kabul is named after her.

Students of Amina Fedawi Girls' High School in Kabul

Resources:

Afghanistan on the corse of History of Mir Ghulam Mohammad Ghobar

Aziz al-Dain and Kayli Popalzai, author of Timur Shah-Durrani

The Role of Women in The Affairs of the Country, Mohaqiq Abdul Rahim Bakhtiani

The Life of Amir Dost Mohammad Khan, The Second Volume by Mohhan Lal De Kandahar.

Professor Rashad, his arrangement ودپتولنه و Simon Mohammad Masoom Hotak, Da Afghanistan de Caltouri. Jermini.2007

Cobra Mazhari, poets and O LikvalanoTazkiras.

[1] Professor Abdul Hai Habibi, A Concise History of Afghanistan, 1989

Academician Azam Sistani, Remembrance of Brave Afghan Women

CHAPTER THIRTEEN

Role of Women during the Second Anglo-Afghan War

Introduction:

Afghan women played very effective roles in the Second Anglo-Afghan War. However, during the First Anglo Afghan War, fearing defeat, the British politicians tried their best to reduce the active role of women in the liberation of their country. According to a contemporary Afghan researcher, Dr. Najib Barakzai, "*Burqa or Chadari was the custom of a Punjabi Hindu tribe who covered their women from top to toe, fearing possible attacks by their enemies. The British brought this custom to Afghanistan in order to weaken the position of Afghan women in the national resistance. The custom of wearing burqa is not mentioned in the Islamic Sharia (Law). However, it was promoted by the strict Deobandi School.*" [8]

The Deobandi school of thought was established in India in 1866 when Great Britain was in control of the Indian subcontinent. After the First Anglo Afghan War, the notion of wearing burqa was widely promoted by the followers of the Deobandi school of thought in Afghan villages. It is not known if the British India politicians were directly involved in this process, but the claim is made more valid in the illustration of James Rattary, a British military artist who came to Afghanistan in the mid-19th century. James Rattray's illustration clearly shows a Kabuli young woman in a typical Afghan traditional costume at the focal point of

Afghan Women by James Rattary, late 1830,
British Library

---

[8] *Dr. Najib Barakzai, The Position of Women in the History and Social Life of Pashtuns Afghan German Online January 2014*

his illustration in contrast with a lady wearing a Burqa in the background. She is standing in a corner, almost resembling a ghost. The artist smartly compares the two styles of clothing for Afghan women, the main style in the foreground and the lady in the Burqa who had just entered the scene from the right corner. It is said that during the uprising of Kabul against the British forces in 1842, Mohan Lal, the British informant and intelligence officer, escaped Kabul wearing a Burqa. Although this report is not officially documented, it seems that British spies and secret envoys were wearing burqas to avoid being caught by the Afghan resistance warriors since Afghans traditionally did not body search women.

According to many researchers, restrictions on women in the Islamic countries increased during the era of European colonialism. It was a natural reaction of the Muslim men to protect their women against the assaults and raids of European soldiers. These restrictions were initiated by men to defend their honor. However, in the second half of the 19th century, there were two points of view in the Islamic countries in this regard. While the followers of the Deobandi and the Wahhabi schools of thought severely restricted women's active role in society, the moderate Muslim scholars such as Said Jamaluddin Afghani, and his close friends and followers as well as moderate Islamic scholars of Turkey thought otherwise; they believed that the only way for Muslim women to compete with the colonial European powers was to promote education and in particular education of Muslim women.

In the late 19th century and beginning of the 20th century, Mahmoud Tarzi, a young Afghan intellectual, who is considered the father of modern journalism in Afghanistan, met with Said Jamaluddin Afghani and became a keen promoter of women education in Afghanistan.

During the Second Anglo Afghan War (1878 -1880), there were still heroic women who stood against British aggression in their homeland and bravely fought for Afghanistan's independence.

Bibi Almasa Ghazi Adeh

Her name was Almasa, nicknamed Ghazi Adeh, (the Victor and Conqueror Mother). She was a tall, strong and very decisive lady. She fought alongside the famous resistance leader, Mohammad Jan Khan Wardak against the British army in Logar Province. She became very famous after the battle of *Sang e Noshta* in the south of Kabul on the way to Logar. In this surprise attack, Bibi Almasa along with 160 women ambushed an English brigade and defeated them. She participated in many battles between (1878 and 1880), including the battle of *Koh-e Gorugh*, the combat of *Qal'a Gazi* and the fight of *ChaharAsyab*. Her most famous battle, however, was the Battle of *Asmaie* inside the city of Kabul. In this famous battle, she led a team of 400 warrior women who fought very bravely against the highly equipped regiment of the British Army. Tragically, along with 80 other brave women, Bibi Almasa was killed in this battle.

Commemorative poster in Honor of Bibi Almasa and Her Counterparts

Almasa was born circa 1835 AD in the Katawaz municipality of Ghazni Province. She belonged to the SulaimanKhail tribe and was a married woman when she fought against the British in the 2nd Anglo Afghan in 1878. When the British forces attacked the southern regions of Afghanistan, both Almasa and her husband, Habib Aka were providing food and ammunition for the Afghan resistance fighters. They had a daughter named Shaista. Out of respect, some villagers would call her the mother of Shaista and some would call her Bibi Almasa. When she became experienced enough to lead the battles and gained the respect of her compatriots, she was given the title of *Ghazi Adeh*, the Victor and Conqueror Mother.

During the reign of King Amanullah (1919-1929), it was believed that Ghazi Adeh was buried in Karte Parwan district of Kabul. The King built a midsize white marble monument in her honor. However, according to Professor Reshad, no one knows her exact burial location since she was killed alongside 80 other ladies at the foothills of Asmaie Mountain and no one had a chance to bury them properly. In her honor, a well-equipped Girls' High School has been named in the city of Kabul.

Malalai, the Heroine of the Maiwand Battle

Malalai is one the most famous and celebrated Afghan women who fought for the cause of Afghanistan independence. She was a modest village girl born in 1861 in Maiwand, a small village on the outskirts of Kandahar. The daughter of a shepherd, Malalai was still in her youth when the 2nd Anglo Afghan war broke out. In November 1878 during the reign of Queen Victoria, 50,000 highly equipped British troops attacked Afghanistan due to political conflict between the British Raj (British India Government) and King of Afghanistan, Amir Shi Ali Khan. While 10,000 Afghans freedom fighters were engaged in a fierce battle against British forces in Kabul, Field Marshal General Robert deployed Brigadier-General George Burrows to attack Kandahar and fight against Prince Ayub Khan who had started an arm resistance against the British occupation from Herat. This was the era of the Great Games between the British Empire and Russian Tsars.

Away from and unaware of the vicious political competitions of world colonial powers, Malalai, a 19 years old free-spirited young girl lived a happy simple life. She was engaged to a young man from her village. She had poetic talent and wrote about the beauty of nature. On July 27th of 1880, her life suddenly changed. The cannons started to fire. There was fire and smoke all over the Maiwand battlefield. In the heat of the month of July, the Afghan resistance fighters were getting shot one after another. They were thirsty and bleeding to death. Malalai and other women of the nearby village were bringing pitchers of water to help the wounded as the British cavalry and foot soldiers were shooting at the Afghan freedom fighters led by Prince Ayub Khan. Malalai was desperately running back and forth to help the wounded. The British army with continued gunfire and heavy artillery changed the battlefield to a burning hell. Many Afghans were getting killed one after another and hundreds were wounded. Under the rainfall of bullets, Malalai saw that her fiance, who was carrying the Afghan flag, was shot. Malalai ran towards her fiance, but he was taking his last breath. She looked at her dying fiance with extreme sadness but also with pride. She grabbed the flag from his hand and bravely ran in front of the Afghan army while encouraging the Afghan fighters to fight to the last drop of their blood in defense of the motherland. Malalai led the battle against the mighty British army in a desperate campaign. Her courage and her reciting patriotic poems on the battlefield boosted the morale of the Afghan fighters. The Afghans ambushed the English army so strongly that they started to retreat while suffering heavy casualties. In the picture below, the British painter Richard Caton Woodville depicted very vividly the British Army's Royal Horse Artillery were defeated and withdrew from this battle.

A view of Maiwand Park in Reading, England

The British army officers were astonished by the bravery of this young Afghan girl who led the war like an experienced general. Unfortunately, as she was advancing toward the British army, Malalaiwas struck by an array of bullets and ultimately died. The story of the great British army's casualties in the Battle of Maiwand, which left behind 969 of British soldiers dead, became a topic of serious discussions in London. Meanwhile the bravery of a young Afghan girl, who fought like a lioness in this battle, became famous in Europe. Subsequently, English and other Western writers referred to her as the Joan of Arc or Jeanne d'Arc of Afghanistan. The story of Malalai is not only told by Afghan historians but also by many Western writers such as Brian Glyn Williams, Eiic Wagner and Howard Hensman who have elaborated on her heroism, bravery, and leadership in the Battle of Maiwand.

The inscription on the pedestal

The significant casualties for the British Army, especially the death of 258 top English military officers and 329 high ranking officers belonging to Queen Victoria Regiment, was considered a great tragedy that left an emotional scar for many people in England. To commemorate those who lost their lives in the Battle of Maiwand, a park called the Maiwand Park was designated in the city of Reading.

A monument in the center of the park has engraved names of the soldiers who lost their lives in the battle. A large bronze lion statue created by George Siminds, a prominent English sculptor, is an important feature of the park. This dark statue depicts the lion's painful roar.

George Simonds committed suicide after completing his famous artwork. Apparently, he personally knew most of the officers who lost their lives in the battle of Maiwand.

Similarly, the memory of Malalai, the heroine of Afghanistan, is still cherished by the Afghan people.

The Maiwand Lion in the Forbury Gardens, Reading England

In a way, the statue of the Lion of Maiwand in the city of Reading and the memory of Malalai's sacrifice in the battle of Maiwand symbolically connect the human sentiments between the two distant and distinct cultures.

Lady Aisha, Daughter of Sardar Afzal Khan

Despite all hostilities during the reign of Amir Shir Ali Khan, cultural activities increased and the Shams al-Nahar news paper was published in Kabul in 1873. Among the literate and knowledgeable women of this era, the most dedicated was Lady Aisha, the daughter of Sardar Afzal Khan. In addition to being a skilled writer and an eloquent speaker, she was an intellectual and an accomplished calligrapher, creating attractive inscriptions with utmost artistic beauty. It is said that she set up a small school for young girls in her private home and taught them how to read, write and recite the Holy Qur'an. Lady Aisha was a kind woman who introduced young girls to moral principles and faith in God.

During the Afghans and British war of 1879, Lady Aiesha helped Afghan fighters and hired doctors to treat the wounded. Highly respected by the king and all those who knew her, Lady Aisha lived until the reign of King Abdul Rahman.

References

Afghanistan on the Course of history, Mir Ghulam Mohammad Ghobar

A Brief History of Afghanistan Pohand Habibi

Sir Arthur Conan DoyleA Study in Scarlet 1887

Groves, J. Percy (1887). The 66th Berkshire Regiment. London:

Headlam, Major General Sir John (1931). The History of the Royal Regiment of Artillery from the Indian Mutiny to the Great War Volume III-Campaigns (1860-1914). Woolwich: Royal Artillery Institution.

Robson, Brian (2007). The Road to Kabul: The Second Afghan War, 1878-1881

Fraser-Tytler, William Kerr (1953) Afghanistan: A Study of Political Developments in Central and Southern Asia Oxford University Press, London,

CHAPTER FOURTEEN

Afghan Women during the Reign of King Abdul Rahman & His Son, King Habibullah

During the reign of King Abdul Rahman, when Afghans and the British coexisted in relative peace, the country was ready for vast developments.

Although Amir Abdul Rahman Khan has been viewed as a dictator, he was a shrewd politician and an efficient administrator. Despite his busy schedule, he always paid attention to women's affairs. King Abdurahman

A View of Bala Hissar Palace

called on scholars of Islam and jurisprudence to define the religious rights of women in accordance with Islamic Law. As a result of this executive order, women became entitled to receive inheritance, and men were obliged to pay alimony in accordance to Islamic regulations. Although women had not yet achieved full freedom, Amir Abdul Rahman sought to recognize their rights accorded to them by Islam.

The public mindset, however, was not very receptive to women's movement or their active involvement in national affairs, especially right after the chaos following the Second Anglo Afghan War. Despite the public's resistance to women's involvement in national or social affairs, under the guidance of Amir Abdul Rahman Khan, Ayesha Durrani's poetry book was published in Kabul Press. Ayesha Durrani's poetry collection was the first book to be published independently by a female author. Although some

fanatical elements secretly objected to these developments, fearing Abdul Rahman Khan, no one dared to express their opposition publicly.

Crown Queen Bibi Halima

Bibi Halimeh was the powerful wife of King Abdu Rhaman. She has been described as an authoritative, resourceful, and courageous lady by Afghan historians. She assisted her husband on many governmental affairs. Often when the king went on trips, she would represent him and attend to important administrative duties in the capital. She performed her role as a decisive queen with confidence and ingenuity. Everyone, including the King, would intentionally give her difficult tasks to resolve, and she would usually succeed in her duties.

Portait of Queen Halima, King Abdul Rahman's wife

Queen Halima was the daughter of Mir Atiqullah and the descendant of Mir Wa'ez Kabuli, a prominent religious scholar. On her mother's side, she was related to King Dost Mohammad Khan. As a young girl among the noble families of Kabul, she was famous for her poise, beauty, and intelligence. Halima was born in 1849 on a rainy day in the city of Kabul. Upon return from Bukhara to Kabul, Amir Abdul Rahman heard praises of her from many different people. Thus, the powerful monarch wanted to know her personally. According to academician Sistani, the contemporary Afghan historian, she was introduced to the king by Prince Sardar Mohammad Yusuf Khan, son of the late king, Amir Dost Mohammad Khan. Abdul Rahman Khan was so impressed that he proposed to marry her although she was only 17 years old. Halima responded in the affirmative but with a condition; that is, she asked the king not to give her a dowry or any material gifts. Her lack of interest in material things impressed the young king even more. Instead, he presented a bouquet of daffodils to her, and Halima responded that this thoughtful gesture of the Great Sultan will always be in her heart and mind.

When Halima officially became the queen, she wore a crown during her visits outside the Royal Palace. A unit of her special guards would always follow her, but she had so much dignity that no one dared to look her straight in the eyes. She was so popular among the common people that they would call her the Crown Queen.

And sometimes out of love, they would call her "Bobo Jaan" (Dear Mother) or Dear Crown Mother Queen although she was not an elderly lady.

During her husband's reign, despite a series of formal agreements with the British, there were still anti-British sentiments among Afghans. Queen Halima also condemned colonialism and wrote poems vouching for independence. Although from a literary vantage point Queen Hamima's poems didn't achieve the sophistication present in Ayesha Durani's verses, they conveyed her deep patriotic feelings and her desire for Afghanistan's total independence.

Queen Halima was extremely interested in the construction of gardens and palaces, and King Abdurrahman admired her even more for her enthusiasm in this field. Since she was very dear to him, he always accepted her proposals for new projects. The royal palace and the charming garden of Bustan Saray, now referred to as Zarnegar Park, located in front of the Arg (palace), was built upon her request. The tomb of Amir Abdul Rahman Khan is also located in this park.

A View of Zarnigar Park and the Mausoleum of King Abdurahman
Kabul, Late 19th century

It should be noted that most gardens in Kabul, including Babur Garden, Shahrara Garden, Mahtab Bagh, and Jahan Ara Garden were all built by women because of their great interest in creating beauty. These gardens show the good taste of Afghan women in different periods of history and their dynamic nature to build their country despite all difficulties caused by wars. Queen Hamia also paid attention to the development of other cities. Following the footsteps of Queen Gawhar Shad, she provided valuable gifts to the museum of the Fourth *Caliph Ali Ben Abi Talib's* Mausoleum in the city of Mazar-e Sharif. She built a bridge between Kabul and Paghman, which is still called the "Halima Bridge". It is believed that this bridge was initially, built by Queen Khadija, but it was totaly destroyed as a result of wars. Thus, Queen Halima rebuilt it. Atthe request of the queen, a magnificent and beautiful palace was built in thenew city of Kabul, still referred to as the palace of Shah Bobo Jan. However, some historians believe that it was built by the request of the king's sister whose name was similar to the queen. In any event, with 40 exquisitely decorated halls, the palace was built to the test of an influancial lady by Austrian engineers in Neo-Classical European style. This shows the importance of women in the construction of splendid palaces and charming gardens in in the late 19th and ealy 20th century.

The Charming Queen's Palace in Kabul

It now houses the Ethnographic Museum of Afghanistan. A number of German and Austrian engineers assisted in this process, and the construction of the Queen's Palace was the responsibility of the Austrian engineers.

The interior decoration of this majestic palace is in the elegant style of nineteenth century Europe. It is created with the most harmonious colors, which reflects the choice and artistic vision of a tasteful woman.

The mosque referred to as Shah Bobo Jan Mosque or the Queen Mother's Mosque, built next to the palace, is still standing intact.

At the request of Queen Halima, King Abd al-Rahman built an additional palace in Babur's Garden known as the Queen's Palace. This mansion is independent of the old building that was built during the reign of Babur by Queen Bibi Mobarakeh, the wife of Zahir al-Din Babur. It can be said that this garden is a testament to the love of two powerful kings for their wives, that is, Zahiruddin Babur and King Abdul Rahman, the most oppressive monarchs whose armies feared them but their love and respect for their queens would not allow them to say "No" to them whenever they asked for something. Both kings fulfilled the wishes of their wives by adding to the beauty and splendor of their historic gardens. Queen Halima lived until the reign of her grandson, King Amanullah. Despite her old age, she continued to promote women's education, and she even donated her residential palace in BostaanSaray to the first girls' school - Masturat - in Kabul.

Queen Halima's Palace in Babur Garden

Afghan Women during the Reign of King Habibullah

After the death of King Abdul Rahman in 1900, his son King Habibullah Khan, titled as *Siraj al-Melatwa al Deen* (The Light of Nation & Religion) became the king of the country. At that time, not only in Afghanistan but in most Eastern countries, including Ottoman Turkey, Egypt, Iraq, Saudi Arabia, and the court of the Qajar kings of Persia, having harems with numerous women was a common practice among kings and powerful men.There were many women in Amir Habibullah Khan's harem, most of whom were interested in poetry and learning.

During this period in Kabul, a considerable number of educated and knowledgeable women lived inside the royal harem and outside the Royal Palace who were acquainted with Islamic studies and common knowledge of that era.

The Harem of King Habibullah

On the other hand, some of the educated women made it their moral duty to promote literacy and bring positive changes in the country. Thus, they would choose teaching, which was and still is considered an honorable profession.

On the order of King Habibullah some of these women were hired to teach at the harem to help educate the princes, princesses and the ladies in the royal palace.

At the end of the nineteenth century and the beginning of the twentieth century, European cultural aspects were slowly finding their way into Eastern countries, including European fashion for the ladies of harem of Amir Habibullah Khan. As well, during the reign of Amir Habibullah Khan, opulent palaces were built in European styles, adorned with the most beautiful Victorian-style furniture and precious paintings.

In this era, workers, especially the high ranking government officials who had to go to the royal palace were required to wear Western style attire; they would usually wear the most luxurious clothes. King Habibullah's keen interest in and sole focuses on fashion and superficial changes disappointed a great number of the country's intellectuals and educated youth. They were against the absolute power of the monarch; demanded social justice; and were focused on bringing about a constitutional monarchy. Some of the Harem women were also supporters of this movement, and one of them was Queeb Sarwar Sultan.

Her Majesty Queen Sarwar Sultan

One of the most influential and powerful women of this period was Queen Sarwar Sultan, the mother of King Amanullah. She came from a powerful clan of Kandahar. The backing of this influential family was very important for strengthening King Habibullah, since the Kandahari influential families played an important role in the politics of this era.

Queen Sarwar Sultan had great authority in the government of King Habibullah. However, in spite of her great power, Queen Sarwar Sultan did not agree with her husband's style of ruling. While she could not change her husband's ways of thinking, as a brave and freedom-loving individual, she worked instead with libertarians and constitutionalists, for whom she had a great deal of sympathy and supported their causes for the creation of a constitutional monarchy.

She was very interested in political and social affairs and wanted her son Prince Amanullah to be the embodiment of the concept of development of freedom and equality in Afghanistan. When Prince Amanullah was only 12 years old, Amir Habibullah Khan named her "Supreme lady of all the ladies". She was the official queen of Afghanistan despite the fact that there were many ladies in the king's harem. As an influential queen, she became more involved in the affairs of the country.

Her son, Prince Amanullah, was born in Paghman, on the outskirts of Kabul, which allowed the young prince to become more familiar with the Kabul environment. But the Queen would take him on frequent trips to Kandahar to acquaint him with that province and his relatives in Kandahar.

Queen Sarwar Sultan was very much interested in the education and advancement of women. She tried to improve the status of Afghan women. During this time, many women who lived outside the royal palace showed great interest in receiving formal education and gaining adequate knowledge. During her reign, like the women of other cities, such as Balkh, Herat, Kandahar, Badakhshan and Ghazni, the women of Kabul were very interested in poetry. Reading poetry books such as Shahnamah, collection of Bidel poems, and Rumi's poems was a common practice among women. Religious themes were important subjects as well.As an enlightened queen, Sarwar Sultan was a great supporter of female education and encouraged her son prince Amanullah in this regard.

Bibi Sangi Afghanistan's First Female Constitutionalis

Bibi Maryam, who later became known as Bibi Sangi, was born in Kabul in 1864 in a middle-class, enlightened family. Her father Sangi Mohammad, known as Ghazi Sangi Baba was from the Sadat dynasty of Kunar. He was one of the most famous fighters in the first Afghan-British war. Maryam's mother, SeyedaAnar was related to the family of Seyyed Abbas Pacha who were descendants of Seyyed Ali Termezi, nicknamed as Pir Baba. He was a religious figure who had many devotees among the people of Kunar, Swat and Khyber.

When Bibi Sangi became an adult, she began to write revolutionary poems, particularly in support of the first constitutionalist movement. Her poetry criticized dictatorship and absolute system of governance. Her revolutionary poems appreciated the freedom movements and condemned British colonialism. She supported intellectual movements in favor of constitutional monarchy. Because of her support for political causes and strong criticism of the Amir's authoritarian methods of governance, Maryam became the target of conservative courtiers. Her sharp tongue along with the courtiers' desire to please and flatter the king caused her serious problems, including imprisonment, which was ordered by the royal court's secretary, Mirza Mohammad Hussein. Although her husband, Haidar Ali Ahrari, was an employee of the Amir's court, Maryam's arrest could not have been prevented. Along with her, many intellectuals were imprisoned as well. Since at that time prisons for women did not exist, KingAbdurahman ordered that she be sentenced to house arrest. However, Mirza Mohammad Hussain, the State Prosecutor, suggested that a small prison be built for her. He got the approval from the king and in a matter of days; he built a separate jail for her in the western section of Kabul. Bibi Sangi was transferred to this stone structure for her jail sentence. The jail was called "Kota-e Bibi Sangi" (Bibi Sangi's Chamber) in the official documents of that era, and later became known as "Kota-e -Sangi" for short. Presently, "Kota-e Sangi" encompasses a large section of Kabul. It extends from Kabul University to the western outskirts of the capital, and it is one of the most populous and developed areas of Kabul.Bibi Sangi was released from prison as a result of the intervention of benevolent people such as Sultan Mohammad Mir Monshi and the guarantee of her husband. When King Habibullah assumed power, he pardoned Bibi Sanji, who then became more involved in the education of children and mostly taught young girls of the royal family. The new king's brother, Amir Nasrullah Khan who had a poetic nature, had high regards for Bibi Sangi's knowledge and her special talent in poetry.

During the reign of Shah Amanullah, Bibi Sangi had earned a high status because of her political stance, her free thinking, and her struggle for independence. When King Amanullah and Queen Sorya established Masturat Girls School) in the early 1920s, she was one of the first ladies to teach in that school. According to contemporary author and scholar, Dr. Asadullah Sha'our, currently two Maryam High Schools in two different parts of Kabul have been named in her honor. These schools were established in her memory to show respect and the level of admiration for her among the people.

A View of Today's Kot- e Sangi

Makhfi Badakhshi

Makhfi is a famous poetess of this era. She was a descendant of the Badakhshan Amirs but spent her childhood in Kabul and Kandahar. It is said that her father, Mir Mahmoud Shah, had to come to Kabul for political reasons during the reign of King

Abdul Rahman. Her father was also a poet but didn't have the chance to publish his work. Makhfi was about eight years old when she lost her father. She was raised by her mother and two elder brothers.

Makhfi's brothers, Mir Mohammad Ghamgin and Mir Sohrab Sawda, also had a poetic talent. It is obvious that Makhfi earned her poetic talent from her family who were familiar with Dari literature. In her 20s she went to Badakhshan during the reign of King Habibullah Khan and settled in the village of "QaraQoz" to learn more about her parents' province.

Makhfi's real name is Sayyed Nasab Begum, but as it appears from her poems, she was also called Ziba al-Nisa. However, in the Encyclopedia of Afghanistan, her first name is mentioned both as "Seyyida" and "Sayyed al-Nasab".

Although most biographers have written that her birthplace is the city of Faizabad in Badakhshan, some historians believe that she was born in the city of Khulm in Balkh province in1879 AD. Makhfi started writing poems in her youth when she was sixteen. As a young girl, she composed optimistic verses. In the beginning, most of her poems were full of feminine emotions about her fiancé Sayyed Mushreb. However, after the death of her beloved fiancé at a young age, her poems became sad and melancholy. She also wrote about the hardships and difficulties she experienced in life.

At first, she kept her poems to herself, but then she began using the pin name Makhfi, meaning Hidden or Secret to conceal her identity.

The first collection of her poems called "*Lal Para Ha*" (Rubi's Pieces) was published in Kabul Literary Magazine, which attracted the attention of the prominent poets and writers of the time. This was the beginning of her career as an eloquent poetess.

This poem in Dari appeared was published in Kabul in the early 20th century. In it, Makhfi discusses life and her beliefs in a stylish and expressive manner.

143

Makhfi did not seek fame or status although the name Makhfi Badakhshi is a familiar name to the people of Afghanistan. Everyone liked her poems and empathized with her broken soul. She is highly respected among the literary circles of the country. During her lifetime, she wrote many verses.

Some of her poetry was recorded in her book, *Chahar Bagh*, (Four Gardens) which is no longer available in the markets. According to the research of contemporary writer Latif Nazemi, there are about 65 sonnets and 22 quatrains, and a number of scattered verses in the collection left by her. In light of his research, we discover that Makhfi Badakhshi, who had spent a life of hardship as a woman poet in a patriarchal society, wrote the following about women's liberation to Ms. Nafisa Shayeq, the editor of Women Magazine:

"Now that I have reached the age of eighty, I am fortunate to be alive and to observe the results of the aspirations I have nurtured for years in the advancement of women's education."

Makhfi had a long life and lived until the reign of King Zahir Shah when she died in 1968.

Mastura Ghori

Hur al Nessa Mastura was the daughter of Mir Said Azam Ghori, who had great interest in Sufism. She was born in the Purchaman (Green Village) district of Ghor circa 1832 AD. Mastura was undoubtedly an accomplished poet and was capable of writing complex verses in classical style with a high level of sophistication. She had a *Diwan* (Poetry Book) with 3,500 verses. It was titled *"Tahfat al-Ashqin Mafrah al-Muslimeen"*(The Gift of Lovers, Happiness of Muslims). However, since she lived in the remote district of Ghor province, she was not very well known in the large cities. Not until her death at the age of 36 was much attention paid to her talent; her name was left out of most of the country's press. She was buried in the "Mountain of Zore," in Ghor Province, her favorite place. In her writings, she praises Zore Mountain's splendid beauty and considers it a legendary mountain, mentioned in ancient fables.Mastura had a simple mystical life. Her spirituality earned her the respect of the local people, who referred to her as the Saintly Lady. After the death of MasturaGhuri, Mahjoba who was greatly inspired by her, continued to write poetry.

Mahjoba Herawi

Safura, konown as Mahjoba Herawi was an eloquent and articulate poetess of this era. She was born in Badghis in 1906 and moved to Herat when her parents chose Herat as their place of residence. Herat was a promising city in which to grow. It was the city of poets, scholars, intellectuals and artists. As a child, she became acquainted with the rich cultural environment which impressed and impacted her immensely. In her teens, her poetic nature started to blossom and gradually became known as a new poetess in a city that was the cradle of arts and literature.

Her original name was Safura, and later she chose the nickname Mahjoba. Safura came from a middle class family. Her father, *Abu al Qasem*, worked as a secretary for a general named *Ghawth al-Din Khan Ghori* during the reign of King Abdu al-Rahman. Mahjoba began writing poetry at the age of 14. Obviously at this age, her poems expressed the thoughts of a young girl with much hope in life.

Mahjoba was gradually was be coming famous. It is said that Masturaheard about Mahjuba's talent and sent her one of her poems. Having seen Matura's style of writing, Mahjuba would write poems following her style but would choose her own topics and send them to her.

The master poetess loved her poems and encouraged her to write more. After the exchanges between the two, Mahjoba took poetry more seriously and started to write at a professional level. She continued to be in contact with Mastura whom she considered as her teacher and mentor.

Her literary nature was flourishing every day, until her family arranged for her to marry a man by the name of Mirza Ghulam whom she had never met before. Mirza Ghulam was a harsh and close-minded man, not at all interested in arts and literature and in particular, disliked women who wrote poetry.

He believed that it was a disgrace to society if a woman expressed her feminine feelings and heartfelt emotions. But young Safura still wanted to write her poems, so she chose the pseudonym Mahjoba to compose poetry, and she became known by this new name. She lived in the old city of Herat, in Mirza Ghulam's house which was surrounded by thick mud walls. She felt as if she was a prisoner living in this house, similar to a bird being inside a cage.

The melancholy verses that she wrote during this period express her state of mind and lack of freedom. They represent the stories of hundreds of other women like her who couldn't express themselves in a male-dominant society. It is said that during her life with Ghulam Mirza, Mahjoba Herawi dealt less with the press, but after her husband's death, she had a more active presence in the Afghan press and poetry circles.

Below is one of her letters written to the Kabul Literary Society:

"I am grateful to the Kabul Literary Association for resolving many issues related to poetic techniques. I dearly thank the scholars of my homeland for helping me. I know I am still in the process of learning and need to improve my knowledge of poetry. I was unable to complete my studies due to many personal problems and being attached to my husband.

After my father's death I didn't have anyone to teach me the intricacies of writing poetry. Therefore, my only teacher was the articles in newspapers, yearbooks, and magazines that came to me.

I live in a house in the old city of Herat, which is older than the city itself. I have lived here like a prisoner, completely unaware of the world outside. Now I want to awaken the people, especially the women until, with the help, God's freedom prevails."

In her poems she explains how trapped she felt, living in confinement and how much she wished to travel in the open fields and feel the breeze of freedom.

Mahjoba Herawi's *Diwan* (poetry book) was published in 1948 by Mohammad Alam Khan Ghawas. Some literary observers compare her poems to those of Rabi'a Balkhi, whose death was caused by the oppression and prejudice of her proud brother just as Mahjoba suffered from the cruelty and prejudices of her husband toward women. Mahjoba had great respect for Makhfi Badakhshi, since she felt her pain.

Despite all limitations in the lives of women, some ladies continued to be active during the reign of King Habibullah.

Maryam Sorkhabi

One of the intellectuals of this era was Maryam Osman, who later in the country's press became known as "Maryam Sorkhabi". Her family members were all highly educated. For political reasons, they moved from Faryab,in northern of Afghanistan to Kabul during the reign of Kin Abdul Rahman.

Maryam Sorkhabi was the wife of Mohammad Osman Khan and the sister of the famous Afghan artist Ghulam Mohammad Musawer, also known as Maimangi. During the reign of King Abdul Rahman, when Ghulam Mohammad Khan was still a young man, he was noted for his great talent in drawing, and learned the Western style of painting from an Englishman named John Gerry, who was a physician and an accomplished artist himself in the court of King Abdul Rahman. He introduced his sister Maryam Osman to Amir Habibullah and his brother Amir Nasurullah to teach their daughters reading and writing and the history of Islam.Maryam Sorkhabi lived with her family in the old city of Kabul. She married Osman King Habibulla's court's confidant during her tenure as a teacher at the royal palace.

A Newspaper cutting from Seraj Al-Akhbar,
Showing the Students of Masuturat Girls' School, Kabul, 1923
Researched by Said Qasim Reshtia, Afghan Historian

147

She had two sons and three daughters, all of whom were educated and had artistic inclinations.Sorkhabi worked with the wife of Mahmud Tarzi, an official who had just arrived in Kabul from Turkey. Both ladies focused on improving educational opportunities for Afghan women, especially young girls. Alongside these two ladies, there were many other educated women who worked for this noble cause as well. Due to a lack of written records, most of them remain unknown.

During the reign of King Amanullah, Maryam Sorkhabi became one the first official female teachers who taught at Masturat Girls' School, teaching history of Islam and writing skills. After the collapse of King Amanullah's reign, she continued to teach but in private girls' school in the royal palace of Nader Shah.
During the reign of King Zahir Shah, she established the "Stouri" Girls' School in Maymana, the capital of Faryab province, in collaboration with Mamlakat Banu, a disciplined and knowledgeable woman. When Maryam Sorkhabi retired, she returned to Kabul, and after a long and fruitful life, she passed away in 1969 and was buried in Kabul.

Resources

Taj al-Tawarikh Volume 1 and 2: Omari Accidents, Travelogs and Diary
 From 1747 to 1900, author Amir Abdul Rahman Khan
Feiz Mohammad Kateb Hazara Siraj al-Tawarikh
Mir Mohammad Sediq FarhangAfghanistan in the Last Five Centuries by
Afghanistan on the Path to History by Mir Ghulam Mohammad Ghobar
New Society of Poets and Writers of Afghanistan Website
Mundigak Afghanistan History Site Dr. Asadullah Shour
Dupree, Louis Abd al-RaḥmānKhān (1980). Afghanistan.
Princeton
Bayes (15th ed).
Articles of Said Qasim Reshtia Afghan Promanent Scholar

CHAPTER FIFTEEN

Women's Movement during the Reign of
King Amanullah and Queen Soraya

The plans for change that had been laid during the reigns of Amir Shir Ali Khan, King Abdul Rahman, and King Habibullah came to fruition in the reign of Shah Amanullah and Queen Soraya.

In the time of King Habibullah, many learned women from various parts of Afghanistan, including Herat, Kandahar, Kunar, Nuristan, Balkh and Faryab had come to Kabul to study traditional subjects such as religion and literature. However, with the arrival of Mahmud Tarzi, his wife and his daughter, Queen Soraya, new ideas entered the traditional society of Afghanistan.

Mahmud Tarzi, who had become acquainted with Sayyed Jamaluddin Afghan in Turkey in the last months of his life, believed strongly in the development of education. His goal was to free the

King Amanullah &Queen Sorya, 1924

eastern countries from the grip of colonialism and backwardness. His erudite wife Asma RasmiaTarzi and his daughter, Soraya Tarzi who later became the queen of Afghanistan were in accord with him.When the young sophisticated Soraya married the progressive Prince Amanullah, it was during their time in power that the liberation of Afghan women was officially proclaimed.

The first step in this period was the publication of *"Irshad al-Nasswan"* (Women's Voice) publication in March 1921 as the first Afghan women's magazine published by Kabul Press. The founder and director of the publication was Asma RasmiaTarzi. Her secretary was Ms. Roh-afza. During this time, fourteen printing houses became active in Kabul and other important provinces of Afghanistan. In addition, seven hundred thousand volumes of textbooks were published throughout the country at the very beginning of Shah Amanullah's reign, which was unprecedented in the history of Afghanistan.The participation of women in educational affairs and

government departments without any discrimination was officially declared in the
Loya Jirga (National Assmebly) of 1922 and adopted in the constitution of
Afghanistan.

The First Issue of Women Magazin & Picture of Mrs. Rasmia Tarzi

Queen Soraya attended the Loya Jirga without wearing the veil or burqa. Several of
King Amanullah's sisters also attended the important session without wearing veils.
This courageous act was unprecedented in other Islamic countries, with the exception
of Turkey and Syria. During this period, for the first time, great changes were taking
place, mainly resulting from Queen Soraya's progressive efforts. The most important
decision during this period was the elimination of harems and abolishment of
slavery, which offered women the opportunity to live free lives. At this time,
Afghanistan was a pioneer in this area since this tradition still existed in most of the
Eastern countries, including Afghanistan's neighboring countries.

The second important step in this period was the establishment of girls' schools for
the advancement and progress of women. At the opening ceremony of the Masturat
School in Shahr-Ara Garden in Kabul, Queen Soraya addressed the audience, who
were mostly women:"

*"Today is a great and hopeful day for the children of our nation who can benefit
from this school, which will enable them to serve their religion, country, and people
to the fullest possible. Those present here know that both men and women are
equally entitled to an education. This school has been established for us women by
the pro-education young king Ghazi Ammanullah Khan, and I appreciate the hard*

work of the Minister of Education in this regard. It is upon us women to work hard to attain knowledge and education."

The second school for girls named Esmat was opened toward the end of 1921 under direct supervision of Queen Soraya. This school was located in BostaanSaray, and was later rebuilt and renamed as Malalai High School, not too far from its original location. A school for adults' literacy was also established, which many women attended. In 1928, the Women's Support Association was founded under the leadership of King Amanullah's sister, Ms. Kobra. In the same year, the Second Loya Jirga was held in Kabul, with more women participating. In this Loya Jirga, Queen Soraya addressed the nation. One of the statements from her speech was as follows:

"Anyone who believes in God and accepts Prophet's Mohammad's message is a free human because God has created all mankind free and religion is not a factor to limit humans.

The statement sparked a stir among a number of fanatical elements in Kabul, demanding Shah Amanullah to divorce Queen Soraya. But Queen Soraya was not afraid of these threats and did not change her position. Instead, with full dignity, she decided to improve the health facilities of women. Under the management of PrencessSiraj al-Banat, she opened the Masturat Hospital, still operational in Kabul. In addition to health-related services, the facility offered elementary, secondary, and high school classes.In 1928, King Amanullah and Queen Soraya traveled to Turkey and Europe. Queen Soraya was one of the first queens of the East to attract the attention of the Western press in Europe. In particular, her interview with the Paris-based magazine Hello further added to her fame and popularity.

King Amanullah and Queen Soraya in Berlin

151

In her interview, she responded with poise, politeness, and dignity to the most difficult questions of the French journalist. The representative of Hello magazine in Paris wrote the following about her:

I have had many interviews with queens and women of first-class officials, but I have rarely seen a woman with the sobriety and ingenuity of the Queen of Afghanistan.

One of the most important actions of Queen Soraya in Kabul was the opening of the Minaret of Knowledge to demonstrate her fight against Ignorance.

*Historical image of Queen Soraya on the official opening day
of the "Minaret of Knowledge and Ignorance"*

This historical monument shows the victory of education over the darkness of ignorance and illiteracy. On the day of the official opening of this symbolic monument, Queen Soraya emphasized the importance of learning, acquisition of knowledge, and gaining education in Islam. She added extra emphasis to the importance of women's education since literate mothers raise literate children.

Another important undertaking of Queen Soraya and Shah Amanullah was the transformation of private gardens to public gardens. Mostly in the past, the big gardens were the recreation area of the kings, the rich, and the powerful. She changed most of the royal gardens into public gardens. Queen Soraya believed that healthy resorts were very important for the growth and morale of children and families and should not be monopolized by the privileged few. Hence, the most beautiful garden of Paghman was officially called Paghman Public Garden; whichuntil today is open to everyone.

Paghman Public Garden, During the Reign of King Amanullah

In 1929, a number of high school girls were sent to Turkey for higher education where they specialized in medicine and health education. Having female physicians was an important issue in the country, since Afghan women were deprived of adequate health services for, they could not be examined by male physicians. However, such important programs and progressive thinking of the King and the Queen were premature and short-lived in a traditional Islamic country. All these innovative steps to improve the conditions of women caused disturbances among the conservatives and resulted in the fall of this progressive government.

The memories of King Amanullah and Queen Soraya, however, are still in the hearts and minds of the nation. Although the 10-year period of this progressive movement ended in 1929, the initiation of such services and the innovative thinking of King Amanullah and Queen Soraya paved the way for civil society, education for all, and the preservation of women's rights in Afghanistan. They served as the foundation for future developments and further liberation of Afghan women.

The first group of Afghan girls to obtain higher education in Turkey

Resources:

Malala Musa Nezam Osaf First Ladies in Afghanistan 2019

M Eskenazi French historian of Afghan women, education and social activities in the Amani era

Shirin Naziri (March 2, 2011). "History of the Women's Movement in Afghanistan" ,Dr. Senzil Naweed ,Religious Response to Social Change in Afghanistan 1919-29 King Aman-Allah and the Afghan Ulama

EncyclopædiaIranica (Online ed.), Columbia ."AMĀNALLĀH" .Poullada, L. B University

Afghanistan: A Short History of Its People and Politics. United ,Evans, Martin Kingdom: CurzonPress

CHAPTER SIXTEEN

Afghan Women from Mohammad Nader Shah's Reign to the First Republic, (1929-1978)

So far, we have documented the activities of Afghan women from the beginning of human life to the era of King Amanullah and Queen Soraya who commenced a movement for women's rights in the early part of 20th century.

The women introduced in this study have left a positive mark in the course of history. As the historical records indicate, these brave women brought about major constructive and transformational changes in society despite all the challenges they faced. But Afghan women's constructive efforts did not stop with the end of the Amani's enlightenment movement. Rather, this progressive movement, which started at the beginning of the 20th century, continues to impact lives of current day Afghanistan. The work and impact of current day Afghan women are so vast that a separate book can be written on their achievements.

After the fall of King Amanullah in January 1929, all the schools were shut down, particularly those of girls' until Mohammad Nader Shah assumed power in November of 1929, when schools for boys opened again. Girls' schools were still blocked. While King Nadir Shah was in favor of reopening the girls' schools, as a prudent politician he was more careful not to provoke the conservative elements who were against women's education and believed that a woman's place was only in the home.

Thus, two years later in 1931 when he saw the timing appropriate, he decided to open a girls' school inside the Royal Palace. He recruited the teachers and the high school students from King Amanullah's era to teach in this palace school. For security reasons, the school had to be inside the royal palace.

In this experimental school, students were learning Islamic studies, history, reading and writing, grammar, arithmetic, geography, drawing, netting and tailoring. Later, when the attitudes toward women's education gradually changed, the teachers and graduates of this school became teachers in the country's other schools.

155

During this time, the *Historical Society of Afghanistan* was established and with the active participation of top Afghan scholars, Kabul Magazine was launched. These important sources provided a great opportunity for the acquisition, accumulation, and spread of knowledge. The literate women benefited from these academic publications immensely. Many literate women enjoyed reading the informative publications of this era, in particular the two daily newspapers, *Anees* and *Islah.*

After a period of uncertainty during the short reign of King Nader Shah, the cultural environment had gradually changed in favor of improving women's social status.

During the reign of King Mohammad Zahir Shah (1933 to1973), further positive changes occurred in women's social life. The most important was the reopening of girls' schools in different parts of Kabul and major cities around the country. A large number of the graduates of these high schools continued their higher education.

Malalai High School was one the first girls' schools that opened in Kabul, followed by Zarghuna, Ayesha Durrani, Rabiae Balkhi, AmenehFadawi, and Bibi Mehro high schools. Additional schools included Princess Belqis and Shah Dokht Maryam high schools and many more all over Kabul and other provinces.

King Zahir Shah and the Active Afghan Women of 1960s

During this era, the government funded education for all levels, kindergartens, primary, secondary and high schools. In both boys' and girls' schools a variety of subjects were covered, including social sciences, biology, chemistry, physics, algebra, geometry, trigonometry, logic, philosophy, Dari and Pashto literature, religious studies, art, and foreign languages. The increase in the number of schools throughout the country prepared thousands of students for college education, which was also funded by the government. Economics, law, and medicine were among the first fields chosen by university-bound female students. During Prime Minister Mohammad Daud's government in1959, women's liberation and the removal of the veil began.Princess Belqis, Princess Maryam (Shah Dokht Maryam), high-ranking women officials of the government, and enlightened women of Afghanistan attended the veil removal ceremony. This took place without any significant incidents in complete security and was widely welcomed by Afghan women.

In 1964, the Afghan constitution approved equal rights for both Afghan men and Afghan women. This constitutional amendment allowed women to serve in all governmental offices and functions, including the cabinet and parliament (Senate and National Assembly). In the 1960s and early 1970s, Afghanistan was one of the first Eastern countries whose women held senior positions in the judiciary, the legislature, and the executive branches.

A Group of Kabul University Students at Kabul University in the 1970s

This era opened gates of co-education, economic progress, sports, and artistic

activities for Afghan women who were able to join their male counterparts at Kabul University, pursuing their education in diverse fields such as engineering, medicine, journalism, history, geography, economics, pharmacy, literature, arts, humanities, law, political science, agriculture, science, and Islamic studies. Foreign languages were also taught at different departments of the university. The government funded not only the students' education but also provided for them room and board if they were from the provinces. After graduation from the university, men and women were offered government posts in appropriate divisions of the government without any gender descrimination.

Flight attendants of Ariana Afghan Airlines, Kabul Airport 1961

Afghan women were active in all walks of life, including the press and in radio broadcasts. Many female avantgarde writers published political commentaries, prepared reports for radio and newspapers, and produced valuable scientific essays. In the field of broadcasting and programming, they presented literary programs,

short stories, novels, screenplays, and acting and produced meaningful theatrical pieces. Women's contributions were meaningful, impactful, and awakening.

During these years, the Women's Institute was opened, offering literacy courses for women, and *Mirmon Magazine* (Women' Magazine) was founded as the official publication of the Women's Center. This cultural center had a cinema, theater and concert hall, named *Zeinab Nandarai*. In addition to showing movies and dramas, famous singers and musicians also performed in this center.

The Family Planning Association was also established during this period. Its goal was to advise young mothers to raise healthy children. The Mother and Child Clinic was an important department of the center. The graduates of nursing schools and healthcare services in the clinic were mostly women.

Public Health Workers (Mother & Child Clinic)

Also, female doctors in the field of general health, preventive medicine, and gynecology were in charge of the Mother& Child Clinic who provided adequate support to economically disadvantaged mothers and children.

Princess Maryam at the Graduation Ceremony of Narsing School

During the 1970s, scholarships for distinguished male and female students increased in different areas of higher education.

Kabul Universty Students at Faculty of Mdecine During 1970s

Afghan students continued their higher education in Afghanistan, and in many friendly countries abroad, working on masters and doctoral degrees in various fields. Upon return, they provided valuable services to the country. Physical education also received great attention during this period; young Afghan girls participated in most team sports such as volleyball, basketball, and skiing. Participation in sport activities was one of the favorite pastimes of young girls and boys in high schools across the country.

During the reign of Mohammad Zahir Shah, Afghanistan became a constitutional monarchy. The constitution protected the citizenship rights of all Afghans, men and women. Queen Homeira accompanied the king on many of his official trips to foreign countries. She was a popular queen and her poise and dignity was praised in the international press.

Jacqueline Kennedy's sister, Queen Homaira, King Zahir Shah and John F. Kennedy during the King's visit in the United States in 1963

During King Zahir Shah's trip to the United States, the friendly relationship between Afghanistan and the United States of America was reinforced. As a result of this visit, more US economic aid was promised for Afghanistan's development. Given her great desire for promoting education, especially for the Afghan women, Queen Homaira's goal was to strengthen the educational relationship between the countries.

Similarly in King Zahir Shah and Queen Homaira visit to Japan, the Afghan queen's role was admired by the Japani's press in establishing a more positive and constructive diplomatic relation between Japan and Afghanistan.

*Tokyo, 1969, the Japanese Imperial Family hosting
King Mohammad Zahir Shah and Queen Humaira during their trip to Japan*

The long and uneventful rule of King Mohamad Zahir Shah, which lasted for four decades, ended on July 17 1973, by the White coup d'etat, led by his cousin Mohamad Daoud. Mohamad Daoud was Prime Minister and a prominent member of the Afghan Royal family. However, due to political differences, he seized power, while the king was in Rome for medical reasons.

The Era of Mohammad Daud's Presidency

President Daud's rule lasted from (1973-1978). One his main goals were to empower the young Afghan generation. During his time in office women become more active in participating in governmental affairs and work in the private sector.

President Daud was one of the founders of the women's liberation movement in the 1950s and instrumental in the removal of the veil in accordance with Sharia law. His policy in regard to women's rights increased active participation of women in all walks of life. During his presidency, Afghan women made further progress in administrative, social, and cultural affairs.

President Daud Khan and a number of women activists in the 1970s

Accordingly, large numbers of Afghan girls traveled to Europe, Asia, and the United States for higher education in various academic fields. For the first time during this period, women were hired by the police forces and the military. Women participated in different sectors of the economy, including owning their own businesses.

A great number of women writers, university professors, cabinet members, and social activists participated in Afghanistan's development that brought about positive changes in the country. During President Daud's reign Afghan National Television was founded. Many women became involved in the fields of television, television programing, video-journalism and news

Afghan Lady Radio Technician

casting. Meanwhile a large number of women started to work in areas of print journalism, photojournalism, storytelling, and video and audio recording and editing. They received their training at a very high professional level. Also courses for television broadcasting became available for both men and women.

At the same time, the Fine Arts branch of Kabul University was established, offering courses in the fields of painting, sculpting, art history, and design. The strong support of the government allowed an unprecedented large number of young Afghan girls to participate in various branches of Fine Arts. After completing their education, these artists trained more students in various fields of art in other major cities such as Balkh, Herat, Kandahar and other provinces.

In the 1970s, with the help of the United Nations (UNESCO) and the Government of Afghanistan, the Rural Development Program was launched. The main goal was to establish literacy courses in remote towns and villages of the country.

In the area of economic development, Afghan women have been engaged in carpet weaving, tailoring, and embroidery for centuries. During this era, further steps were taken to provide self-employment opportunities for rural Afghan women. Villagers in remote areas of the country received special vocational development training programs to prepare themselves for work in economically profitable fields.

During the presidency of Mohammad Daud, a large number of women began to work as doctors, nurses, judges, engineers, diplomats, public speakers, athletes, filmmakers, movie stars, theatrical performers and singers.

Following Daud Khan's assisination and the period of political turmoil and wars that ensued (1978 to 2001), Afghan women were the biggest victims of these events. In the month of April 1978, the Moscow backed regime seized power in Afghanistan, which was followed by Soviet invasion of the country in December 1979.

During these hostile times, in spite of all the difficulties and hardships, the Afghan women coped with new harsh realities of life. Many women were killed and forced to flee the country, and money lost their spouses and loved ones. After the communist regime came to power, thousands of Afghans, mostly women and children, became homeless as a result of wars and destructions. They became refugees in neighboring countries and all

over the world. From the years 1978 to 2001, poverty, disease and mental stress affected the people of Afghanistan, especially women and children. During this period, Afghanistan had the largest number of widows and orphans.

After a long period of war and distruction, Afghan women had a chance to play an important part not only in advancing their family lives but also in helping the country move forward.

A Carpet Weaver lady from the village of Aqcha, Northern Afghanistan

Subsequent to overthrow of the Taliban regime by NATO forces, 2001 was the beginning of a new era of development in Afghanistan. The Bonn Agreement stipulated that the rights of Afghan women must be restored. The goal was that Afghan women, whose rights we violated during the wars, should be protected from further aggression. Under this agreement, the United Nations and NATO countries declared their support for Afghan women. The new constitution of Afghanistan approved on January 4, 2004, in accordance with the guidelines of the religion of Islam and the moral standards of the Afghan society, guaranteed the right of women to participate in all economic, political, and social activities without discrimination based on their merit. The new constitution approved by LoyaJerga (the National Assembly) enshrined the rights of Afghan women in several articles.

The constitution of 2004 gave full civil rights to Afghan women, allowing them to participate in all three branches of government as well as actively work in the private sector. Additionally, the provincial council, which had 420 seats, had 124 seats for women. Since 2001, Afghan women have been participating in the presidential as well as local elections. This participation was estimated at 42 percent, which is higher than in most Eastern countries. The establishment of "Afghan Women's Network" during these years, promoted women's economic and cultural activities to a higher percentage as reported by the Afghan government.

Afghan Women Farmers

This network consisted of institutions and foundations headed by women. The activities of the "Afghan Women's Network" in different parts of the country promote education and culture and defend the rights of women. The Ministry of Women's Affairs was established to enhance the social and educational development of women. The main goal of this Ministry was to improve the social status of women and create positive working conditions for female students and women in general throughout the country. Parallelling the Ministry's efforts, the Women's Development Fund was established by the United Nations in 2007 to end violence against women. At the same time, a number of non-governmental organizations (NGOs) began working to protect the rights of Afghan women in general.

As is well known, Afghan women have had extensive experience in agriculture dating back to a distant past. Accordingly, they have been very successful in producing saffron, which has been ranked, in terms of its quality, as the best worldwide.

Similarly, the handicrafts commonly produced by women are valuable contributions to the national economy. The statistical data of 2010 shows that the new opportunities for women led to significant progress in the country.

The number of girls' schools increased by 31%, the number of primary schools increased by about 40%, and the number of universities in Kabul and other provinces increased by 19%. This increase is about 15% in non-governmental educational institutions.

Between 2001 and 2021, Afghan women played very important roles in the political arena, including participation in the legislature, judiciary, and executive branches. Afghan women worked as diplomats, United Nations delegates, ambassadors, cabinet members, and members of the parliament. Research shows that under the right circumstances, Afghan women are exceptionally competent in all walks of life, including managing and/or being involved in businesses and economic development projects. In terms of their progress in education, Afghan women's achievements have been impressive, particularly in the field of engineering, medicine, scientific fields, computer technology, and journalism (radio and television). According to Rest of World, an international nonprofit journalism organization, Afghan Girls' Computer Robotics Team was among the top 30 scientists and inventors in Asia in the field of computer inventions.

Afghan Computer Robotic Team members

In 2016, BBC, reported that The Afghan Girls' Robotics Team built the first artificial respiration device. It was considered a great scientific achievement in the country, which shows the rich talent of the young generation of Afghanistan. The Afghan Girls' Robotics Team was founded in 2017 by Roya Mahboob, Afghanistan's first female tech CEO in the city of Herat.

Also, the resourceful young Afghan girls founded The Dreamer Institute in Kabul to educate the youth from across the country. As Devi Lockwood, assistant editor at Rest of World writes, *"Members of the team wanted to start their own companies, become engineers, and even go to Mars."*

Also, the initiatives of young Afghan girls in the field of culture and fine arts improved greatly from 2008 to 2012. The innovative paintings of the young Afghan girls attracted the attention of art lovers worldwide. They exhibited their paintings in most countries of the world. These young artists tell many untold stories in their paintings; their clear thoughts carry messages of peace and freedom not only to Afghans but to the rest of the world.

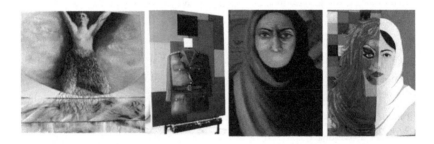

Afghan Women Paintings, Slating the Present Social & Political Situation

These paintings reflect the current state of affairs of Afghan women in the country and demonstrate the artistic genius of the young, female Afghan generation.

Likewise, in the field of music, allegory, filmmaking, writing, poetry and literature in all the languages of Afghanistan are praiseworthy.

In recent years, after the Afghan Youth Classical Orchestra, most of whose musicians are young girls, has attracted so much world attention that there are fewer examples.

Afghan Female Musicians

Afghan women have also achieved remarkable success in the field of competitive sports at the national and international levels, including soccer, volleyball, taekwondo, skiing, karate and wrestling. As well, in the military and security fields, the presence of female officials had become more and more prominent.

Afghan Women Taekwondo Team

Afghan Girls' Soccer Team,

Afghan Women Soldiers

Although there are still problems and threats to the progress and development of Afghan women, dating back throughout history, we come to the conclusion that the brave and talented women of the country have overcome immense obstacles over and over again.

With courage and the support and cooperation of their male counterparts, forward-looking Afghan women will make the necessary progress and bring about peace and freedom in the country.

An Assembly of Afghan Women in Kabul

Today, after decades of war, we discover that Afghan women have made extraordinary progress in the political, cultural and social development of Afghanistan since 1919. Their contribution to the country's economic growth as well as their participation in all aspects of life show a steady level of progress despite all the challenges faced during decades of war and various regime changes. The obstacles of a traditional society have not stopped them from playing a significant role in their country's development.

Their active participation from early epochs until the modern era is a reality which shows their impact on Afghan culture, art, literature, education, and economy in general and their lasting role in the country's liberation and independence as an independent state in different historical periods in particular.

171

With great courage and side by side with men, Afghan women today are active in restoring civil rights for women so that once again they can be active participants in the country's reconstruction, independence, and progress (economic, cultural, social, political, and scientific) and are working hard so that peace and freedom can prevail once again .

Apandex

Afghan women's participation in the social and cultural progress and economical grouth has been isntialthrout the ages. In today's market Afghan women products such as carpetweaving, kneting, sewing, embroidery and wonderful handicrafts including making most auntic jewelry has a lot of admieres around the globe. Here I am eclosing some examples of these fine products that have their orignnality.

Afghan Women Carpet Weavers from Northern Afghanistan

Afghan Rug Turkman Design

Young Girl in Turkman Drsss

Kandahari Embroridery

Embroidered Horse Covering and Bridle,

Northern Afghanistan

Afghan Pillowcase Embroidery

Katawz Dress

Afgha Handmade Dress from Siuthern Afghanistan

Authentic Afghan Jewlery

Made in the USA
Monee, IL
13 August 2023

40789678R00105